Acting Edition

Ernxst,
Or the Importance of Being

Book by
Justin Elizabeth Sayre

Lyrics by
Kait Kerrigan

Music by
Bree Lowdermilk

Based on
The Importance of Being Earnest
by Oscar Wilde

Copyright © 2025 by Justin Elizabeth Sayre, Kait Kerrigan,
and Bree Lowdermilk
Artwork © 2025 Subplot Studio
All Rights Reserved

ERNXST, OR THE IMPORTANCE OF BEING is fully protected
under the copyright laws of the United States of America, the British
Commonwealth, including Canada, and all member countries of the
Berne Convention for the Protection of Literary and Artistic Works, the
Universal Copyright Convention, and/or the World Trade Organization
conforming to the Agreement on Trade Related Aspects of Intellectual
Property Rights. All rights, including professional and amateur stage
productions, recitation, lecturing, public reading, motion picture, radio
broadcasting, television, online/digital production, and the rights of
translation into foreign languages are strictly reserved.

ISBN 978-0-573-71134-3

www.concordtheatricals.com
www.concordtheatricals.co.uk

FOR PRODUCTION INQUIRIES

UNITED STATES AND CANADA
info@concordtheatricals.com
1-866-979-0447

UNITED KINGDOM AND EUROPE
licensing@concordtheatricals.co.uk
020-7054-7298

Each title is subject to availability from Concord Theatricals Corp.,
depending upon country of performance. Please be aware that
ERNXST, OR THE IMPORTANCE OF BEING may not be licensed by
Concord Theatricals Corp. in your territory. Professional and amateur
producers should contact the nearest Concord Theatricals Corp. office
or licensing partner to verify availability.

CAUTION: Professional and amateur producers are hereby warned that
ERNXST, OR THE IMPORTANCE OF BEING is subject to a licensing
fee. The purchase, renting, lending or use of this book does not constitute
a license to perform this title(s), which license must be obtained from
Concord Theatricals Corp. prior to any performance. Performance of
this title(s) without a license is a violation of federal law and may subject
the producer and/or presenter of such performances to civil penalties.
Both amateurs and professionals considering a production are strongly
advised to apply to the appropriate agent before starting rehearsals,
advertising, or booking a theatre. A licensing fee must be paid whether
the title(s) is presented for charity or gain and whether or not admission
is charged. Professional/Stock licensing fees are quoted upon application
to Concord Theatricals Corp.

This work is published by Concord Theatricals Corp.

No one shall make any changes in this title(s) for the purpose of production. No part of this book may be reproduced, stored in a retrieval system, scanned, uploaded, or transmitted in any form, by any means, now known or yet to be invented, including mechanical, electronic, digital, photocopying, recording, videotaping, or otherwise, without the prior written permission of the publisher. No one shall share this title(s), or any part of this title(s), through any social media or file hosting websites.

For all inquiries regarding motion picture, television, online/digital and other media rights, please contact Concord Theatricals Corp.

THIRD-PARTY MATERIALS USE NOTE

Licensees are solely responsible for obtaining formal written permission from copyright owners to use copyrighted third-party materials (e.g., incidental music not provided in connection with a performance license, artworks, logos) in the performance of this play and are strongly cautioned to do so. If no such permission is obtained by the licensee, then the licensee must use only original materials and materials that the licensee owns and controls. Licensees are solely responsible and liable for clearances of all third-party copyrighted materials, and shall indemnify the copyright owners of the play(s) and their licensing agent, Concord Theatricals Corp., against any costs, expenses, losses and liabilities arising from the use of such copyrighted third-party materials by licensees. For music, please contact the appropriate music licensing authority in your territory for the rights to any incidental music not provided in connection with a performance license.

IMPORTANT BILLING AND CREDIT REQUIREMENTS

If you have obtained performance rights to this title, please refer to your licensing agreement for important billing and credit requirements.

ERNXST, OR THE IMPORTANCE OF BEING was commissioned by the Educational Theatre Association and presented in a staged reading sponsored by Concord Theatricals at the 2022 International Thespian Festival in Bloomington, Indiana on June 24, 2022. The production was directed by Justin Elizabeth Sayre, with music direction by Zachary Orts. The stage manager was Sydney Stephenson. The cast was as follows:

JAX	Jasmine Iacullo
ALGY	Christopher Nguyen
CECILE	Mel Driggers
GWYN	Alexis Helmer
LADY BRACKNELL	Jeron Robinson
WINCE	Kara Cody
SPERANZA	Sophie Littig
OSCAR	Lukas Freeman
FINGAL	Hayes Hunter
WILLS	Trinity Hines
WILDE	Eva Parhami
O'FLAHERTIE	Lauren Betz
ENSEMBLE	Rylee Armstrong, Madelynn Atkinson, Lucia Graves, Sofia Jones, Annie Sullivan, Maddie West, Landon Small, Cam Ramirez, Sam Pepper

CHARACTERS

PRINCIPAL

JAX – (20s) Dignified and steady on the surface, yet underneath Jax is a bundle of nerves. Jax is a young person searching for their place in the world. Jax hopes to maintain a certain decorum in order to win love and respect in society. Always walking a self-imposed tightrope, Jax longs for order, while around every corner encounters only confusion and strife. Jax is the emotional center of the show, and their journey toward self-acceptance is paramount to the show's success.

ALGY – (20s) Jax's best friend. With a mischievous grin, Algy flouts the rules of society. A scamp and a bit of rogue, Algy is always having the best of times no matter the company or the circumstances. Algy's a clown discovering that underneath it all there's a heart in need of love.

CECILE – (18) Jax's young ward. Young and vibrant, Cecile is looking out on the world with hopeful and expectant eyes. A person of enormous imagination and drive, Cecile weaves journals and notes into a history of who and what this "Cecile" may actually become.

GWYN – (20s) Jax's Love. Gwyn has been raised to be the jewel of society. Seemingly prim and proper to all, Gwyn has an uncovered depth. A young person confined by society, Gwyn looks to Jax as a way out. In Gwyn, we someone constrained by the role they play in society, or rather, the role they are asked to play.

LADY BRACKNELL – (50s) Jax's obstacle. A Lion of the social order. Dignified and pompous, with an often unintended wit. Bracknell stands for the right way things are done and the right people doing them. Bracknell is the final word in style, society, and ultimately the happiness of most of the people in our play. Lady Bracknell should have a classic, aristocratic British Accent (RP).

WINCE – (40s) The leader of our "Wildes," Wince is the taskmaster in charge of making sure that this play about manners is done with the utmost correctness and sense. A stern leader, Wince is dire even in moments of hilarity. A deadpan face of no in a world screaming out with yes!

SLOUCH – (20s) Wince's assistant. Where Wince is all rules and regulations, Slouch is here for the pure enthusiasm of the theatre. Slouch is awestruck that there's a play going on and in some way, Slouch may actually get to be a part of it. An excitable and ultimately charitable character, Slouch inhabits all our excitement about putting on a show and the power of what it is to be seen.

THE WILDES

Named after the author, these are the makers of our merriment. The Wildes step into any and every role that is required to create the scene, the setting, or the character needed for the play to carry on. They should be played by open and dynamic performers who are able to inhabit even the smallest of moments with wit and personality.

The Wildes are intended to be an ensemble of at least ten performers, but can performed with as few as six and can be infinitely and creatively expanded beyond the named characters.

FEATURED WILDES

OSCAR – Higher Voice with high pop belt and strong upper register

FINGAL – Higher Voice with high pop belt

O'FLAHERTIE – Higher Voice with strong mid-range pop belt

WILLS – Higher Voice with strong mid-range pop belt

WILDE – Lower Voice with high pop belt

SPERANZA – Lower Voice with high pop belt

OPTIONAL ADDITIONAL WILDES

For split tracks – named for important figures in Wilde's life.

CONSTANCE

ELLEN

BOSIE

ROBBIE

In the score, "Wildes" refers to **OSCAR**, **FINGAL**, **O'FLAHERTIE**, **WILLS**, **WILDE**, and **SPERANZA**. "Ensemble" refers to the entire ensemble (non-principals), while "All" means ensemble, featured soloists, and principals.

Casting Note:

While gendered names are adapted or maintained from the original, the spirit of the show is one of exploration. Casting should be based on a performer's embodiment of the character regardless of gender, race, and ability. There are several pre-approved alternate keys for no extra charge. Please refer to your Keyboard-Conductor for a list of the available keys.

MUSICAL NUMBERS

ACT I

Scene One

[MUSIC NO. 01 – BECOME YOURSELF]

(A blank stage.)

*(Slowly, our **WILDES** enter the space, each carrying an object to furnish what will become Algy's sitting room. Each **WILDE** strikes a pose as they deliver their quote.)*

WILLS. "I am not young enough to know everything."

O'FLAHERTIE. "True friends stab you in the front."

WILDE. "I can resist everything except temptation."

FINGAL. "The only difference between a sinner and a saint is…

O'FLAHERTIE. …Every saint has a past

WILLS. …And every sinner has a future."

OSCAR. "Man is least himself when he talks in his own person. Give him a mask, and he will tell the truth."

O'FLAHERTIE. "We are all of us in the gutter…

SPERANZA. …But some of us are looking up at the stars."

*(Enter **WINCE**, 50s, our majordomo of the evening, an exacting servant of the utmost and upright propriety. They are very stiff,*

very sure, very aware of the right way things are to be done. They enter holding a small clipboard with a pencil. While **WINCE** *is lost in lists,* **SLOUCH**, *20s, wanders on behind them.* **SLOUCH** *is a young and rather awestruck enthusiast, taking in the theatre, and even waving to the audience. They're very excited to get started.)*

*(***WINCE*** *stops center, perfectly center, and checks something off the list.)*

WINCE. *(Very stiffly.)* Good evening, gentles all.

SLOUCH. Welcome to the theat-RE.

WINCE. Excuse me?

SLOUCH. I say it with the R-E to be more sophisticated.

WINCE. *(Moving on.)* Tonight, we celebrate the work of –

(The first group of **WILDES** *line up across the stage, to announce themselves and our author.)*

OSCAR. Oscar

FINGAL. Fingal

O'FLAHERTIE. O'Flahertie

WILLS. Wills

WILDE. Wilde.

(The second group of **WILDES** *follow suit.)*

OSCAR. The poet,

FINGAL. Playwright,

O'FLAHERTIE. Novelist, and

WILLS. Lover of...

WILDE. Green carnations.

*(All the **WILDES** pull out a green carnation, and pin it to their lapels.)*

SLOUCH. Green carnations? That's a little queer, isn't it?

OSCAR. You have no idea.

*(The **WILDES** break from their line and begin to assemble the room. **SLOUCH** gets lost in the swirling excitement, as **WINCE** oversees the **WILDES'** construction.)*

O'FLAHERTIE.
WHEN THE LIGHTS ARE LOW

OSCAR.
AND THE DOOR'S SHUT TIGHT

SPERANZA.
YOU CAN TAKE YOUR SPACE

O'FLAHERTIE, OSCAR & SPERANZA.
YOU CAN FIND YOUR LIGHT

*(**SLOUCH** follows after **WINCE** in a state of amazement. Distracted, **SLOUCH** bumps into **WINCE**.)*

WINCE. Slouch!

SLOUCH. I'm sorry, but it's all so wonderful!

WINCE. As it's meant to be. Stop gawping and come along.

*(**WINCE** takes **SLOUCH** off as the **WILDES** continue to construct the room.)*

SLOUCH.
OH OH.

WILDE.
WITH ITS STYLE GENTEEL

FINGAL.
AND ITS MANNERS MILD

WILLS.
COMES THE GAYEST LARK

WILDES.
FROM THE PEN OF WILDE.

(**SLOUCH** *and* **WINCE** *reenter as the* **WILDES** *continue to build the scene.*)

SLOUCH. I feel like that's meant to say something.

WINCE. It did. But you aren't.

(**WINCE** *moves* **SLOUCH** *off, as chairs are moved into place.*)

OH OH.

OSCAR.
LIFE IS WHAT YOU MAKE IT.

SPERANZA.
IF THE SHOE FITS,

OSCAR & SPERANZA.
BREAK IT IN.

(*The* **WILDES** *create Algy's sitting room, in joyous celebration.*)

WILDES.
NO ONE WILL KNOW
IF IT'S YOUR MAKEUP OR YOUR NATURAL GLOW.

WINCE. (*Shouted.*) Let's go!

(*The* **WILDES** *build with abandon!*)

WILDES.
BECOME, BECOME,
BECOME YOURSELF.

FINGAL.
THE WORLD IS WAITING FOR YOUR SELF.

O'FLAHERTIE.
YOU'RE MAKING RAINBOWS FROM YOURSELF.

WILDES.
BECOME, BECOME
YEAH, EV'RYONE,
BECOME, BECOME,
BECOME YOURSELF.

(**WINCE** *reenters with a long rolled-up banner. They hand it to* **FINGAL** *and* **O'FLAHERTIE.**)

WINCE. Tonight, we present Wilde's masterwork.

(**FINGAL** *and* **O'FLAHERTIE** *unfurl the banner which reads, "The Importance of Being ErnXst."*)

ALL. *The Importance of Being...*

(*The scene comes to a halt as everyone tries to understand the typo.*)

WINCE.
SLOUCH!

(**SLOUCH** *reenters.*)

SLOUCH. What did I do?

WINCE. The sign reads "The importance of being 'Ernixst'"? "Ernext"? One barely knows how to pronounce the thing without succumbing to the guttural. Why was I not alerted to this error?

SLOUCH. Oh, because I did it on purpose. You know, X? The unknown. X marks the spot.

(*To audience.*) Who's Ernest? I don't know. Spooky.

WINCE. Ridiculous. I shall deal with you later. For now, let us proceed.

> (**WINCE** *claps twice and the music begins again.*)

O'FLAHERTIE.
> WHEN THE TEA IS POURED
> IN THE PARLOR ROOM,

WILLS.
> THOUGH THE TONE IS LIGHT
> FEEL THE TENSION LOOM.

WINCE. The year is 1893, in a fashionable part of London.

> (*As the room begins to take shape.*)

We find ourselves in the sitting room of Algy Moncrieff.

> (*From stage left,* **OSCAR** *and* **WILDE** *push on the actor playing* **ALGY MONCRIEFF,** *our smiling and beguiling mischief maker. They delight in the drama.*)

OSCAR & SPERANZA.
> OH, OH.

WINCE.
> SUCH A FASHION PLATE
> OH SO DIGNIFIED

SLOUCH.
> HIDING GAMBLING DEBTS
> WITH A BOAST OF PRIDE.

ALGY. Oh, I'm so naughty!
> OH, OH!

WILDES.
> LIFE IS WHAT YOU MAKE IT.
> IF THE SHOE FITS,

BREAK IT IN.
NO ONE WILL KNOW

SLOUCH.

WHAT'S BEHIND THE MASK –

WINCE.

OR SCENIC TABLEAU.

ALL.

OH!

(The **WILDES** *take* **ALGY** *into the sitting room set. They dress* **ALGY** *and place them into the scene.)*

ALGY.

HEIGH HO!

ALL.

BECOME, BECOME, BECOME YOURSELF.
THE WORLD IS WAITING FOR YOUR SELF.
YOU'RE MAKING RAINBOWS FROM YOURSELF.

FINGAL.	**ALL (EXCEPT FINGAL).**
BECOME BECOME BECOME.	BECOME, BECOME, YEAH EV'RYONE, BECOME.

(From the opposite side of the stage, **JAX WORTHING** *enters.* **JAX** *is reserved yet friendly to a fault.)*

JAX.

BECOME YOURSELF.

O'FLAHERTIE. Enter Ernest Worthing, a young person of excellent character,

SPERANZA. ...if slightly faulty pedigree.

SLOUCH. But oh so dreamy.

JAX. That's very sweet, but I'm merely myself.

WINCE. Or that's what you'd like us to think. Come along,
Slouch.

> (**JAX** *flashes a humble smile as the* **WILDES**
> *prepare them for the scene.*)

ALL.
> A COSTUME DRAMA SET
> IN EIGHTEEN NINETY-THREE
> OPENS UP THE WORLD
> OF WHO WE USED TO BE.
> THE DRESSES AND THE SUITS,
> VICTORIAN AND QUEER.
> OUR LIES BELIE A TRUTH
> THAT'S HIDING
> UNDER THE VENEER.

WINCE. We present this paragon of wit, satire...

SLOUCH. And the course of true love!

ALL.
> TIME FOR THE SHOW TO START.

> (**JAX** *and* **ALGY** *are set in the now assembled
> sitting room as* **WILDES** *complete the
> tableau.*)

WINCE. Places, everyone!

ALL.
> PLAY YOUR PART

SLOUCH. Take up your trays!

WINCE.
> LIGHTS UP! LOOK SMART!

ALL.
> BECOME, BECOME, BECOME YOURSELF.
> THE WORLD IS WAITING FOR YOUR SELF.
> YOU'RE MAKING RAINBOWS FROM YOURSELF.

BECOME, BECOME
NOW, EV'RYONE –

WINCE.
WELL, NOT EV'RYONE –

ALL.
OH YES! EV'RYONE!

OSCAR, FINGAL & SPERANZA.	**WILDES.**
BECOME, BECOME	BECOME, BECOME, BECOME YOURSELF
OH BECOME YOURSELF.	THE WORLD IS WAITING FOR YOUR SELF.

ALL.
YOU'RE MAKING RAINBOWS FROM YOURSELF.

(**WINCE** *races around to put the final touches on the room.* **SLOUCH** *is handed a tray of cucumber sandwiches.*)

BECOME,

(**WINCE** *weaves through the scene, giving it a last minute check.*)

WINCE.
SMILES ALWAYS BRIGHT.

ALGY.
OH!

WINCE.
PINKIES ALWAYS OUT.

SLOUCH. (*Looks at sandwiches on tray.*)
SANDWICHES ALWAYS...CUCUMBER?

ALL (EXCEPT OSCAR & FINGAL).	**OSCAR & FINGAL.**
BECOME,	BECOME...

ALL (EXCEPT OSCAR & FINGAL).
BECOME,
BECOME...

WINCE.
THE IMPORTANCE OF BEING...

> (**WINCE** *looks at the banner and gets hung up on the X again...* **SLOUCH** *shrugs.*)

ALL.
YOURSELF!
OH OH.

> (**JAX** *tries to take a sandwich, and* **ALGY** *slaps their hand away.*)

WINCE. And scene!

Scene Two

The Sitting Room

(The majority of **WILDES** *exit, except for a few who play* **SERVANTS** *attending to the grand home.* **SLOUCH** *holds the tray of cucumber sandwiches between* **ALGY** *and* **JAX***, thrilled to be part of the scene.)*

ALGY. *(Taking a cucumber sandwich.)* Please don't eat the cucumber sandwiches! They've been ordered especially for my Aunt Augusta.

JAX. I haven't had one! You've been eating them all this time.

ALGY. I have? Well, so I have but that is quite different. She's my aunt. And Aunt Augusta won't approve of your being here one bit.

> *(***ALGY*** takes a cucumber sandwich and goes to sit down.)*

JAX. May I ask why?

> *(***SLOUCH*** sneaks a cucumber sandwich. They're pretty good.)*

ALGY. The way you flirt with my cousin Gwyn. It's perfectly disgraceful. It's almost as bad as the way Gwyn flirts with you.

JAX. I am in love with Gwyn. I have come up to town expressly to propose to them. I think it's perfectly romantic.

> *(***ALGY*** takes a few more cucumber sandwiches and goes to sit in one of the chairs.)*

ALGY. I don't see anything romantic about proposing. It is very romantic to be in love. But there is nothing romantic about a definite proposal. Why, one may be accepted. One usually is, and then all the excitement is over. But perhaps in this case, there's more excitement to come.

JAX. I don't want excitement, I just want Gwyn.

ALGY. And why wouldn't you? My cousin Gwyn, is a rare jewel in the diadem of society. But as such, the greatest care must be given to their potential suitor. So, before I would ever allow you –

JAX. *Allow* me? Who are you...

ALGY. *(Barrelling through.)* – to propose, I would find it within my cousinly duty to clear up the question of... Cecile.

OSCAR. OOOH! Who's Cecile?

ALGY. *(To* **WINCE**, *offstage.)* Are they going to do that the whole play?

> *(All the* **WILDES** *pop their heads into the scene.)*

WILDES. *(Onstage.)* Yes! We are!

[MUSIC NO. 01A – UNDERSCORE]

JAX. Cecile! What do you mean, Algy, by Cecile? I don't know anyone of the name Cecile.

> **(ALGY** *produces Jax's calling card case from their pocket.)*

ALGY. And yet your calling card case says something quite different.

JAX. Do you mean to say you have had my calling card case all this time? I have been writing frantic letters to Scotland Yard.

(**JAX** *swipes at* **ALGY** *to grab the calling card case, but* **ALGY** *backs away.*)

ALGY. Oh no! You see, now that I look at the inscription, I find that the thing isn't yours after all.

(*They chase each other around.*)

JAX. You have no right whatsoever to read what is written inside.

ALGY. It's absurd to have a hard and fast rule about what one should and shouldn't read. More than half of modern culture depends on what one shouldn't read. This case is a gift from someone by the name Cecile. (*Reading.*) "From Little Cecile, with fondest love." (*Then.*) Now if you don't know someone named Cecile, who could this Cecile be, to have given this to you?

JAX. Well... Cecile...is my auntie.

ALGY. Your auntie! Then why do they call themselves Little Cecile, if they're your auntie?

JAX. Some aunties are tall, some aunties are small. For heaven's sakes, give me back my case!

(**JAX** *tries to take the case, but* **ALGY** *scampers away.*)

ALGY. But this case was given to someone named Jax, and your name is Ernest.

(*They chase each other again, and out of breath,* **JAX** *stops.*)

JAX. (*Spoken.*) Alright. My name is Ernest in town. And Jax in the Country. The case was given to me in the country.

(**JAX** *reaches for the case and again is thwarted.*)

ALGY. By your minuscule auntie?

JAX. Fine! If you must know Cecile is my ward. When my guardian, Old Thomas Cardew, died some years ago, they, in turn, made me Cecile's guardian. And when one is placed in such a position of respect and authority, one must adopt a very high moral tone on all subjects.

ALGY. And to be high and moral one must be called Jax?

JAX. Algy. No, but you see, to protect Cecile, I've made up the tiniest and simplest of lies, really. Cecile's a wild and headstrong young person, with grand ideas of adventure.

ALGY. They sound perfectly marvelous.

JAX. They are. That's why you shall never meet them. I keep Cecile safe and away in the country, where they can live a life of ease and peace. I visit often, and when I am in need of a life away from all that ease and peace, I come to town to look after my sibling, Ernest. Who I made up.

ALGY. You're a Bunburyist! In fact, you are one of the most advanced Bunburyists I know.

JAX. What on earth do you mean?

ALGY. You have invented a very useful younger sibling called Ernest…

> (**ALGY** *looks around and grabs* **WILLS**, *who's been dusting.* **ALGY** *takes a shawl from the set and wraps it around* **WILLS** *and sits them on the couch.)*

…where I too have invented an endlessly sickly friend named Bunbury.

(To **WILLS**.*)* Cough, Bunbury.

> (**WILLS** *coughs.)*

Very good. Bunbury's extraordinarily bad health gets me out of so many of life's more boring obligations. Why just last night, Bunbury's bout of gastric discomfort...

(**WILLS** *is confused as to what to do. What's a gastric?*)

Tummy.

WILLS. *(Moaning.)* Oh, my poor gastric.

ALGY.　Precisely. That little tummy ache gave me the perfect excuse to decline a dreadful invitation last night. I'm sure amongst Bunbury's horrifying list of ailments –

(**WILLS** *acts a fever, a headache, a chill, a heart attack, choking, very quickly.*)

Very good, Bunbury, we can find the perfect excuse to turn down dinner at Aunt August's. I'd much rather go with you to Dorian's and discuss our wickedness.

WILLS.　Am I still sick?

JAX. No, I'm afraid the only sick thing in this room is Algy's mind! To compare my simple and totally reasonable fib, with your continual deceptions is quite beyond the pale. I'm not a Bunburyist, nor never will be. In fact, should Gwyn accept my proposal, I'm going to kill off my sibling Ernest. Cecile is entirely too interested in them at present. And if you had any moral character, you'd bring an end to your Bunbury as well.

(**ALGY** *clings to* **WILLS**, *as if to protect them.*)

[MUSIC NO. 02 – THE SOCIALS TODAY]

(**ALGY** *takes a top hat and a cane and begins their jaunt as a dandy.*)

ALGY.　Nothing will induce me to part with Bunbury! They're some of the most fun I have!

> (**WILDE** *appears, also in a top hat, as a* **BUNBURYING PAL**. *Throughout* **ALGY**'s *solo, more* **WILDES** *step into the space as* **BUNBURYING PALS**, *all in top hats, with canes. They all begin to stroll out, and take space in the room.*)

ALGY.

SEE I DROPPED BY A DANCE LAST NIGHT,

LEFT MY CARD

WITH A NOTE

FOR THE HOST

STOLE A GLANCE,

STOLE A DANCE,

I DO FANCY A CHAMPAGNE TOAST.

ALGY, WILLS & WILDE.

THEN THE NIGHT

COULD BEGIN.

ALGY.

AU REVOIR.

> (**JAX** *gets up to leave and is forced back down by* **WILLS** *and* **WILDE**.)

ALGY, WILLS & WILDE.

HELLO SIN.

ALGY.

I'M A KNAVE.

SO I'LL SAVE THE REST FOR MY MEMOIR.

THE RUMOR MILL STARTS CHURNING

SPERANZA.

SO YOU NEED A PROPER COVER.

ALGY.

THE SOCIAL SET IS YEARNING

FOR THE SCANDAL

OF A LIFE OR LOVER

ALGY & BUNBURYING PALS.
THROW YOUR HANDS UP
THE WORLD'LL HANG ON

ALGY.
CAN'T KEEP UP WITH THE SOCIALS.

ALGY & BUNBURYING PALS.
BANG ON!
FLAGRANTLY FLOUT
THE RULES ON DISPLAY.

ALGY.
CAN'T KEEP UP WITH THE SOCIALS.

ALGY & BUNBURYING PALS.
HEY, HEY,
UH-UH-UH-OH,
UH-UH-UH-OH,

ALGY.
CAN'T KEEP UP WITH THE SOCIALS
TODAY

You see, with Bunbury, I can maintain the good graces of society while allowing myself the freedom to do anything I please!

JAX. I am a serious person, Algy. And serious people don't need a Bunbury. Especially when they plan to marry.

ALGY. Marriage is the perfect time for a Bunbury! You don't seem to realize that in married life, three is company and two is none.

WILDE. What's four?

ALGY. Just getting started!

> (**ALGY** *links arms with two of the* **BUNBURYING PALS. JAX** *comments with skepticism.)*

ALGY.

WHEN THE WORLD TRIES TO PIN YOU DOWN
ON THE HOOK

JAX.

YOUR BLACK BOOK
IS TOO THICK?

ALGY.

YOU DEMUR

JAX.

YOU FLÂNEUR?

ALGY.

I DEFER TO MY FAKE SIDEKICK.

BUNBURYING PALS.

IT'S THE TRICK.

ALGY.

HAVE AN OUT,
HAVE SOME FUN.

> (*The* **BUNBURYING PALS** *surround* **JAX***, and
> try to draw* **JAX** *into the dance.*)

BUNBURYING PALS.

HIT AND RUN.

ALGY.

EXIT GAME.

ALGY & BUNBURYING PALS.

GOTTA BLAME YOUR
FAREWELL ON SOMEONE.

JAX.

THE RUMOR MILL STARTS CHURNING

ALGY.

TIME TO MAKE AN IRISH EXIT?

JAX.

THE SOCIAL SET IS YEARNING

ALGY.

AND A LITTLE TOO MUCH CANDOR WRECKS IT.

ALGY & BUNBURYING PALS.

THROW YOUR HANDS UP,

THE WORLD'LL HANG ON

JAX.

CAN'T KEEP UP WITH THE SOCIALS.

ALGY & BUNBURYING PALS.

BANG ON,

FLAGRANTLY FLOUT

THE RULES ON DISPLAY.

ALGY & JAX.

CAN'T KEEP UP WITH THE SOCIALS.

ALGY & BUNBURYING PALS.

HEY, HEY,

UH-UH-UH-OH,

UH-UH-UH-OH,

ALGY, JAX & BUNBURYING PALS.

CAN'T KEEP UP WITH THE SOCIALS

TODAY.

BUNBURYING PALS.

HEY, HEY, HEY,

HEY, HEY, HEY

> (**ALGY** and the **BUNBURYING PALS** *surround* **JAX** *who keeps trying to get out of their web. Each takes* **JAX**'s *arm in a sort of do-si-do, that gets more and more raucous.*)

OSCAR.

FANCY HIGH TEA AT FIVE?

ALGY.

BUT MY FRIEND'S JUST ARRIVED!

BUNBURYING PALS.

CAN'T KEEP UP!

WILLS.

I'VE A BOX AT THE OP'RA

ALGY.

MY FRIEND'S IN THE VODKA.

BUNBURYING PALS.

CAN'T KEEP UP!

FINGAL.

CAN WE MEET FOR CROQUET?

ALGY.

MY FRIEND'S BIRTHDAY'S TODAY!

WILDE.

WE COULD GRILL

ALGY.

MY FRIEND'S ILL.

SPERANZA.

POKER GAME?

ALGY.

HE'S GONE LAME!

BUNBURYING PALS.

YOU'RE TOO KIND!

ALGY.

I'M RESIGNED.

BUNBURYING PALS.

OH

ALGY.

PLUS IT GETS ME OUT OF EV'RY

BUNBURYING PALS.

OH

ALGY.

BIND!

BUNBURYING PALS.

THE RUMOR MILL STARTS CHURNING

ALGY.

LITTLE BIRDIES HAVE TO TWITTER.

BUNBURYING PALS.

THE SOCIAL SET IS TURNING

ALGY.

BOTTOM'S UP BEFORE THEIR SWILL GETS BITTER.

Why be so many people, when there's so much fun to be had as yourself!

(**JAX** *is overcome in the moment and joins the dance with a hat and cane of their own.*)

ALGY.	**BUNBURYING PALS.**
THROW YOUR HANDS UP,	OH
THE WORLD'LL HANG ON	

BUNBURYING PALS.

CAN'T KEEP UP WITH THE SOCIALS.

ALGY.

CRACK ON,

ALGY & BUNBURYING PALS.

FAFFING ABOUT,

GET CARRIED AWAY.

JAX.

CAN'T KEEP UP!

ALGY & BUNBURYING PALS.

CAN'T KEEP UP

CAN'T KEEP –

WILDES.
THROW YOUR HANDS UP

ALGY & BUNBURYING PALS.
THE WORLD'LL HANG ON

BUNBURYING PALS.
CAN'T KEEP UP WITH THE SOCIALS.

ALGY.
BANG ON!

BUNBURYING PALS.
FLAGRANTLY FLOUT
THE RULES ON DISPLAY.   **ALGY.**
                                HEY, HEY, HEY.
                                HEY, HEY, HEY.
CAN'T KEEP UP WITH THE
  SOCIALS.
HEY, HEY,
UH-UH-UH-OH,
UH-UH-UH-OH,   CAN'T KEEP UP WITH THE
OH   SOCIALS.

> (The **BUNBURYING PALS** put a top hat and
> cane on **JAX**. They're in the group now.)

BUNBURYING PALS.
CAN'T KEEP UP

ALGY & BUNBURYING PALS.
CAN'T KEEP CAN'T KEEP UP
TODAY!

> (The **BUNBURYING PALS** fall back into chairs,
> spent, just as the doorbell rings.)

ALGY. Ahh, that must be Aunt Augusta. Only relatives or
creditors ring in that Wagnerian manner. Excuse me.

JAX. Wait, how do I look?

ALGY. Like yourself. Whomever that may be.

JAX. Be serious, Algy.

ALGY. I won't, thank you. But I will get Aunt Augusta out of your way for ten minutes so that you can have the opportunity to propose to Gwyn, *IF* I may dine with you tonight at Dorian's?

JAX. The food is terrible.

ALGY. Yes, but it looks divine.

(The doorbell sounds again.)

JAX. Fine. Dorian's then. Just hurry.

ALGY. If you're so worried, take a look in the mirror, there are several. One must know one's angles.

*(**ALGY** exits to answer the door.)*

*(As **ALGY** exits, a few of the **WILDES**, dressed in similar clothes to **JAX**, enter as **JAX'S** **MIRROR IMAGES**. **JAX** looks nervously at themself, making sure they are presentable for the arrival of the beloved **GWYN**.)*

FINGAL. You look well, Jax.

JAX. You mean Ernest. We're in town, remember?

WILLS. Of course. How could Algy accuse us of being a whatever that was?

JAX. A Bunburyist. How absurd! Algy just doesn't understand.

WILLS. Well how could they really.

JAX. One has a duty...

OSCAR. ...and one has people who rely on one...

WILDE. ...So in order to be what others need of one...

JAX. ...it is at times necessary for one to become two.

[MUSIC NO. 03 – WIDER SPECTRUM]

JAX. That makes sense, doesn't it?

WILLS.	**WILDE.**	**OSCAR.**
Of course!	Indubitably!	Makes Solid Sense to me!

JAX. And even if it can be...

WILLS. Exhausting and...

WILDE. Jarring and...

OSCAR. Even a little lonely at times.

JAX. Still we do it. Because one has to be someone that people can rely upon. All by oneself.

> SOME WOULD SAY
> A MAN'S FACE IS THEIR AUTOBIOGRAPHY
> A WOMAN'S FACE IS THEIR WORK OF FICTION
> AND MY FACE – MY FACE – MY FACE IS...
> ON A WIDER SPECTRUM
> NEITHER EITHER OR
> CHASING SOMETHING TRUE
> BARELY SHINING THROUGH
> FOLLOWING AN INSTINCT TO AN UNMARKED DOOR,
> TO A WIDER SPECTRUM
> HARDLY EVEN SEEN
> SLINKING IN SO THIN
> WARMING UP THE SKIN
> PROVING THERE'S A WORLD WITHIN WHAT'S IN BETWEEN

(The **WILDES** *surround* **JAX.** *They reach up with* **JAX.***)*

WILDES. WHAT IF YOU OPEN LIKE A RAINBOW?

JAX.

> SOME WOULD SAY
> A MAN'S LIFE IS THEIR
> TOTAL AUTONOMY
> A WOMAN'S LIFE IS A
> CONTRADICTION
> AND MY LIFE – MY LIFE –
> MY LIFE IS...
> ON A WIDER SPECTRUM
> STRETCHING OUT A HAND
> REACHING FOR A SKY
> DREAMING I CAN FLY
> SOMEWHERE I CAN MEET SOMEONE WHO'LL
> UNDERSTAND.

WILDES.

> COME ON AND OPEN
> LIKE A RAINBOW

WILDES.

> AND IF I OPEN LIKE A
> RAINBOW
>
> IF I COULD OPEN LIKE A
> RAINBOW
>
> WILL SOMEONE OPEN
> LIKE A RAINBOW
>
> COME ON AND
> OPEN LIKE A RAINBOW –
> TO ME
>
> WITH ME

JAX.

> AND IF I OPEN LIKE A
> RAINBOW
>
> IF I COULD OPEN LIKE A
> RAINBOW
>
> WILL SOMEONE OPEN
> LIKE A RAINBOW
>
> OPEN LIKE A RAINBOW –
>
> TO LAUGH, TO LEAP,
> TO RUSH IN LIKE A TIDE

JAX.

> TO BRACE, TO BREATHE,
> TO BLUSH IN THE

JAX.

EVER EXPANDING
EVER WI-I-IDER SPECTRUM

WHAT A WORLD TO SEE!
WHAT COULD BE MAY BE.
EVERY PEDIGREE
ALL OF US STILL ACHING
STRETCHING OUT AND WAKING
ALL SET FREE.

WILDES.

AND WE CAN OPEN LIKE A RAINBOW	**JAX.**

THE WORLD CAN OPEN
    LIKE A RAINBOW
	WILL SOMEONE OPEN LIKE
	    A RAINBOW WITH ME?

AND WE CAN OPEN LIKE
    A LIKE A RAINBOW
	WILL SOMEONE OPEN LIKE
	    A RAINBOW WITH ME?

THE WORLD CAN OPEN
    LIKE A RAINBOW
	SOMEONE OPEN LIKE A
	    RAINBOW

OPEN LIKE A RAINBOW	OPEN LIKE A RAINBOW

*(The **WILDES** exit. **JAX** is alone.)*

OH	OPEN LIKE A RAINBOW

Scene Three

(**ALGY** *returns.*)

ALGY. All ready? They're coming.

[MUSIC NO. 03A – UNDERSCORE]

(**WINCE** *enters to announce the arrival. All the* **WILDES** *crowd into doorways and hide behind chairs to get a good look.*)

WINCE. Society has its queens,

the ones who set the scenes,

Well, here are two who wholly imbue

the fabulous with what it means...

(*Calls out.*) The very fine, very dignified...the lovely Gwyn Fairfax.

(*Enter* **GWYN FAIRFAX**, *a beautiful and dignified young person. There's an outer exterior of cool dismissal that masks a deeper fire.*)

GWYN. (*Entering scene.*) Algy.

(*Then very turned on.*) Errrnessst.

(**WINCE** *clears their throat to reclaim the attention of the room.*)

WINCE. An arbitress of grand style,

Who never cracks a smile

She has no doubt who's in or out

She cancels those who dare defile –

(*Calls out.*) Gwyn's esteemed mother, Lady Bracknell.

(*Enter* **LADY BRACKNELL**, *a very regal matron, with a withering manner. Nothing impresses her as much as herself.*)

LADY BRACKNELL. (*Entering into scene.*) Good afternoon, Algy. I hope you're behaving yourself.

ALGY. I'm behaving *like* myself, Aunt Augusta.

LADY BRACKNELL. That's not quite the same thing.

JAX. My word, you're positively gleaming today, dearest Gwyn.

GWYN. I know. I do that.

LADY BRACKNELL. I apologize for our delay, Algy. I was obliged to call on dear Lady Harbury. I hadn't seen her, since her poor husband's death. I never saw a woman so altered; she looks quite twenty years younger.

JAX. (*To* **GWYN**.) You're quite perfect, you know.

GWYN. Oh, I hope not! It would leave no room for developments, and I intend to develop in many directions.

LADY BRACKNELL. And now I'll have a cup of tea and one of those nice cucumber sandwiches you promised me.

(*Three* **WILDES** *enter with tea and bread and butter and* **SLOUCH** *enters with the empty tray of cucumber sandwiches.* **WINCE** *follows, making sure the service is pristine for* **LADY BRACKNELL**.*)

(**ALGY** *goes to the tray of cucumber sandwiches and finds them gone.*)

ALGY. Good heavens! Wince! Why are there no cucumber sandwiches? I ordered them especially.

WINCE. Slouch?!?

SLOUCH. *(Trying to come up with an excuse on the spot.)* Well...this morning...at the market...I was looking for the cucumbers...to make the sandwiches...but...

WINCE. Yes? And?

SLOUCH. There were none. I went twice. Thrice even.

(**WINCE** *gestures to the* **WILDES** *to exit. They all exit)*

ALGY. No cucumbers! What is the world coming to! Oh but, just as one disappointment follows another, I'm afraid I shan't be able to dine with you tonight, Aunt Augusta. My poor friend Bunbury is most gravely ill.

LADY BRACKNELL. *(Suspicious.)* This Bunbury friend of yours seems to be riddled with so many *timely* maladies.

ALGY. Yes, alas poor Bunbury. They never met a germ they didn't like. Or rather a germ who didn't like them.

LADY BRACKNELL. Well, I must say, Algy, I think it is high time that this Bunbury person made up his mind whether he is going to live or die. This shilly-shallying around with the question is perfectly absurd. I should be much obliged if Bunbury, would be kind enough not to take some turn for the worse this Saturday, so you may attend my musical evening.

ALGY. I shall speak to Bunbury, directly. If they're still conscious, of course. But I imagine by Saturday, they should be right as rain. I was actually thinking of the program for your petite soirée musicale.

LADY BRACKNELL. Shall we call it an evening, Algy? I'd prefer to not involve the French before we absolutely have to.

ALGY. As you like, Aunt Augusta. Perhaps I could play you some of my inklings and tinklings in the next room?

LADY BRACKNELL. Thank you, Algy. It is very thoughtful of you.

ALGY. It is, isn't it?

> (**LADY BRACKNELL** *gets up to leave.*)

LADY BRACKNELL. Gwyn you will accompany me.

GWYN. Certainly, Mamma. I shall follow shortly.

LADY BRACKNELL. Gwyn. Now.

> (**LADY BRACKNELL** *exits, followed by* **ALGY** *who gestures to* **JAX** *that now is the time for action!*)

Scene Four

*(***GWYN*** *and* ***JAX*** *are all alone, as the* ***WILDES****
all hide to listen to the lovebirds.)*

JAX. Charming day, isn't it?

GWYN. Pray don't talk to me about the weather. Whenever people talk to me about the weather, I always feel quite certain that they mean something else. Do you mean something else, Ernest?

JAX. I do. I do, dearest Gwyn.

GWYN. I thought so. In fact, I am never wrong.

*(***GWYN*** *sits, and tries to encourage* ***JAX*** *to do
the same.)*

JAX.   And I would like to take advantage of Lady Bracknell's temporary absence.

GWYN. Please do! Mamma is very protective of me. At times, I wish I could split myself in two, one to please Mamma, and the other to please myself.

JAX. You've no idea how it brightens my heart to hear you say that. Oh my darling Gwyn, ever since I first met you I have admired you more than anyone…I have ever met…since I met you.

GWYN. *(Still in the dream of imagining themself as more than one person.)* Yes, but then what if the other me was more beautiful, or slightly more clever, or perhaps garnered more attention in some way? I wouldn't like that. I imagine there's no use in working oneself into a dither about being two people when one is only one.

JAX. Oh, darling Gwyn, you are so wise!

GWYN. I am. And beautiful. And here. Alone. While Mamma is the next room. And can't see us.

JAX. Dear Gwyn.

GWYN. Dearest Ernest.

> (*The* **WILDES** *peek out in a running gag of the show.*)

WILDES. (*Lovey-dovey.*) Ernest.

JAX. (*A bit overwhelmed.*) Yes, that is most definitely my name.

> (**GWYN** *stands up to take charge of the scene.*)

GWYN. I am pleased for it. You see, we live in an age of ideals, and my ideal has always been to love someone by the name Ernest. In fact, the moment Algy first mentioned they had a friend named Ernest, I knew I was destined to love you.

JAX. You really love me, Gwyn?

GWYN. Passionately! Adamantly! Immediately! As in now please!

> (**JAX** *embraces* **GWYN**. *All the* **WILDES** *audibly swoon.*)

JAX. Darling! You don't know how happy you've made me!

GWYN. I do! But you don't know how happy you've made me! My own Ernest!

WILDES. Ernest!

> (**JAX** *pulls away.* **GWYN** *is left on the couch, a little confused and a little more miffed.*)

JAX. But...

GWYN. But? I feel a strange compunction in your conjunction.

JAX. You don't really mean to say that you couldn't love me if my name wasn't Ernest? I don't much care for the name... I don't think it suits me at all.

[MUSIC NO. 04 – EARNEST LOVE]

GWYN. It suits you perfectly. It is a divine name. It produces vibrations.

LOVE BY ANY OTHER NAME, DEAR ONE,
IS IT EVEN LOVE AT ALL?

WILDES.

WHOA-OH-OH-OH.
WHOA-OH-OH-OH.

GWYN.

LIKE A MOTH DRAWN TO A FLAME, DEAR ONE,
WHEN I SAY YOUR NAME, I FALL.

WILDES.

WHOA-OH-OH-OH.
WHOA-OH-OH-OH.

GWYN & WILDES.

WRITTEN IN THE STARS

GWYN.

I WAS MEANT TO FIND YOU.

GWYN & WILDES.

ANYWHERE YOU ARE,
I'LL BE THERE BY YOU.

GWYN.

I FEEL NEW

GWYN & WILDES.

VIBRATIONS UNDER MY SKIN.

GWYN.

I FEEL

GWYN & WILDES.

A NEW HEAT SETTLIN' IN
I'M IN

GWYN.
> EARNEST, EARNEST,

GWYN & WILDES.
> EARNEST LOVE.

O'FLAHERTIE.
> WHOA-OH-OH-OH.
> WHOA-OH-OH-OH.

GWYN.
> EARNEST EARNEST

GWYN & WILDES.
> EARNEST LOVE

WILLS.
> WHOA-OH-OH-OH.
> WHOA-OH-OH-OH.

JAX. But what of the name Jax?

GWYN. Jax?

WILDES. Jax?!!

> *(The music stops.)*

GWYN. No, there is very little music in the name Jax. It produces absolutely no vibrations.

JAX. None at all?

WILDES. None!

GWYN. The only really safe name is Ernest.

WILDES. Ernest.

JAX.
> CALL ME ANYTHING YOU WANT, SWEETHEART.
> I'M A JACK OF ANY TRADE

WILDES.
> WHOA-OH-OH-OH.
> WHOA-OH-OH-OH.

GWYN.
ONLY ONE NAME FOR MY LOVE, SWEETHEART
EVERY OTHER'S A CHARADE.

WILDES.
WHOA-OH-OH-OH.
WHOA-OH-OH-OH.

JAX & GWYN.
WRITTEN IN THE STARS.
I WAS MEANT TO FIND YOU.
ANYWHERE YOU ARE
I'LL BE THERE BY YOU.

JAX.
I FEEL NEW

WILDES.
OH

JAX & WILDES.
VIBRATIONS UNDER MY SKIN.

GWYN.
I FEEL

GWYN & WILDES.
A NEW HEAT SETTLIN' IN.
I'M IN

JAX.
EARNEST, EARNEST,

JAX, GWYN & WILDES.
EARNEST LOVE.

GWYN.
WHOA-OH-OH-OH.
WHOA-OH-OH-OH.

JAX & GWYN.
EARNEST, EARNEST,

JAX, GWYN & WILDES.
EARNEST LOVE.

JAX.
WHOA-OH-OH-OH.
WHOA-OH-OH-OH.

(The **WILDES** *rush around to create the most perfect proposal scene. Flower petals are thrown, and ribbons are strewn around the room.)*

GWYN.	**JAX & WILDES.**
TAKE MY HAND,	EARNEST, EARNEST,
	EARNEST LOVE.

GWYN.
AND GET DOWN ON ONE KNEE WHEN YOU PROPOSE!

JAX.
YOU MEAN NOW?
JUST PROPOSE TO YOU RIGHT NOW?

GWYN.
ONLY IF YOU WANT A PERFECT ROSE.

WILDES.
HERE'S YOUR CHANCE!
THIS IS HAPPENING RIGHT NOW!

(The **WILDES** *create a perfect springtime tableau around* **GWYN.** *They move a flummoxed* **JAX** *into the scene and shove them down onto one knee.)*

RING?

(They produce a ring and hand it to **JAX.***)*

JAX.
YES!

WILDES.

FLOWERS?

*(They hand **JAX** a bouquet.)*

JAX.

YES!

WILDES.

READY?

GWYN.

YES!

JAX.

WILL YOU?

GWYN.

YES!

JAX.

MARRY ME?

ALL (EXCEPT JAX).

YES! YES! YES!

> *(The **WILDES** create a mad swirling celebration. It's a fantasy proposal full of falling petals and confetti, garlands of flowers and ribbons. An idyllic scene, except for **JAX** and **GWYN** getting separated to make it all happen.)*

WILDES.

WRITTEN IN THE STARS.

I WAS MEANT TO FIND YOU.

ANYWHERE YOU ARE

I'LL BE THERE BY YOU.

> *(The **WILDES** move **GWYN** and **JAX** back together.)*

GWYN.
> I FEEL NEW
> VIBRATIONS UNDER MY SKIN.

JAX.
> I FEEL
> THE NEW HEAT SETTLIN' IN.

GWYN, JAX & WILDES.
> WE'RE IN
> EARNEST, EARNEST, EARNEST LOVE

GWYN.
> WOAH-OH-OH-OH.

JAX.
> WOAH-OH-OH-OH.

GWYN, JAX & WILDES.
> EARNEST, EARNEST, EARNEST LOVE

GWYN.
> WOAH-OH-OH-OH.

JAX.
> WOAH-OH-OH-OH.

WILDES.
> WOAH-OH-OH-OH.
> WOAH-OH-OH-OH.
> WOAH-OH-OH-OH.
> WOAH-OH-OH-OH.

GWYN.
> LOVE BY ANY OTHER NAME, DEAR ONE.
> IS IT REALLY LOVE AT ALL?

JAX & WILDES.
> WOAH-OH-OH-OH.
> WOAH-OH-OH-OH.

> > (**JAX** *gets on one knee, and* **GWYN** *sits on their leg!*)

(Applause.)

JAX. I must be christened – I mean we must be married at once!

*(**LADY BRACKNELL** enters.)*

LADY BRACKNELL. What is the meaning of all this foofery! Adjust yourselves from that post-terpsichoral posture!

GWYN. Mamma! I am engaged!

LADY BRACKNELL. Pardon me, but you are not! When you do become engaged, I, or your father will inform you of the fact. And as for you, Ernest Worthing, I have some questions. Gwyn, you shall wait for me in the carriage.

GWYN. Mamma!

*(**GWYN** goes to the door and blows **JAX** a kiss. **LADY BRACKNELL** catches it, squashes it and throws it to the floor.)*

LADY BRACKNELL. Gwyn, the carriage! Now!

*(**GWYN** exits.)*

Scene Five

*(When **GWYN** is out of the room, **LADY BRACKNELL** walks around, inspecting **JAX**, then finds herself a chair.)*

LADY BRACKNELL. Now to our darker purpose. You may be seated, Ernest Worthing.

JAX. Thank you, Lady Bracknell, I prefer to stand.

[MUSIC NO. 05 – BORN WITH IT]

*(As **LADY BRACKNELL** makes herself comfortable, three **WILDES** with frames come into the scene behind her, creating a wall of family **PORTRAITS**. Each portrait should be of a different period and different expressions.)*

LADY BRACKNELL. I shall sit amongst my antecedents. Family being the only true wealth in this world.

JAX. So I have been told, Lady Bracknell.

LADY BRACKNELL. Yes, by myself. Just now.

*(As **LADY BRACKNELL** sings, the **PORTRAITS** act as backup singers ever in approval.)*

BORN TO BE

ENVIED.

YOU KNOW THIS GRADE OF SASS WON'T QUIT.

I LOVE IT.

I NEED THE DRAMA OF IT.

I'M A CLASSIC.

I GOT MORE STOCK THAN MY ESTATE.

YOU WANTED TOTAL CANDOR,

MY STYLE IS MORE MEANDER.

MAKE. YOU. WAIT.

LEISURE'S MY SUIT,

TIME IS NO OBJECT.
STILL AT THE ROOT
YOU HAVE NO PROSPECTS.
CHARMED THOUGH I AM,
YOUR UNBRIDLED HOPE IS QUAINT.

PORTRAITS.
CUZ HONEY YOU AIN'T

LADY BRACKNELL.
BORN WITH IT.

PORTRAITS.
SING IT AGAIN.

LADY BRACKNELL.
BORN WITH IT.

ALL.
CUZ WE KNOW WHEN

LADY BRACKNELL.
YOU'RE

ALL.
BORN WITH IT.

LADY BRACKNELL.
I GOT MY GRANDMOTHER'S NOSE
FOR THE STENCH OF THE CLIMB.
YOU GOT A NOBODY NOSE
FROM AN UNKNOWN LINE.

PORTRAITS.
SURVEY SAYS:

LADY BRACKNELL.
"NOT BORN WITH IT."

PORTRAITS.
LOUDER FOR THE MEZZ.

LADY BRACKNELL.
"NOT BORN WITH IT."

PORTRAITS.
NO-NO-NO NO

LADY BRACKNELL.
YOU GOT A NOBODY NOSE.

PORTRAITS.
NO-NO-NO NOSE

LADY BRACKNELL.
NOBODY KNOWS

So, Worthing, you are not on my list of eligible partners for my dearest Gwyn, and I have the very same list as the Duchess of Bolton. However, I am prepared to enter your name, should your answers be what a really affectionate mother requires. How old are you?

JAX. Twenty-five.

(The **PORTRAITS** *approve.)*

LADY BRACKNELL. I have always been of the opinion that one who desires to get married should know either everything or nothing. Which do you know?

JAX. I know nothing, Lady Bracknell.

(The **PORTRAITS** *approve.)*

LADY BRACKNELL. Good. Ignorance is like a delicate exotic fruit, touch it and the bloom is gone. What is your income?

JAX. Between seven and eight thousand a year.

(The **PORTRAITS** *are impressed.)*

LADY BRACKNELL. You have a townhouse, I hope? Someone with such an unspoiled nature, as Gwyn, could hardly be expected to reside solely in the country.

JAX. I own a house in Belgrave Square.

(One of the **PORTRAITS** *gets very excited.)*

LADY BRACKNELL. What number in Belgrave Square?

(The **PORTRAITS** *are hopeful.)*

JAX. One forty-nine.

(The **PORTRAITS** *are disappointed.)*

LADY BRACKNELL. The unfashionable side. Tell me of your parents.

JAX. I have lost both my parents.

(The **PORTRAITS** *are confused.)*

LADY BRACKNELL. To lose one parent, Ernest Worthing, may be regarded as a misfortune; to lose both looks like carelessness.

YOUR PAST IS
BAGGAGE.
NO DOUBT THE BRAND IS COUNTERFEIT.
NO MERIT.
THE MEEK WILL NOT INHERIT
ANY DIAMONDS.
YOU CAN'T TURN WATER INTO WINE.
AND NOW YOU WANT TO SELL IT?
WELL COME IN CLOSE I'LL TELL IT:

YOU'RE MOONSHINE.

PORTRAITS.
WE'RE READIN' THE *SIGN*!

(They hold up a sign.)

LADY BRACKNELL.
"NOT BORN WITH IT."

PORTRAITS.
SING IT IN FRENCH.

LADY BRACKNELL.
NE ENFANT AISE!

PORTRAITS.
BACK ON THE BENCH!

LADY BRACKNELL.
I'M BORN WITH IT.

PORTRAITS.
SHE'S GOT HER GRANDMOTHER'S TASTE
FOR THE FAMILY WINE.
YOU GOT A NOBODY FACE
FROM AN UNKNOWN LINE.

LADY BRACKNELL.
NEVER DOUBT

PORTRAITS.
SHE'S BORN WITH IT

LADY BRACKNELL.
BUT NO NEED TO SHOUT

ALL. *(Whispered.)*
I'M BORN WITH IT

PORTRAITS.
NO-NO-NO NO

LADY BRACKNELL. And this misplaced father of yours;
who was he?

JAX. I am afraid I don't really know.

> (The **PORTRAITS** *all are disturbed by what
> they're hearing.)*

The fact is, Lady Bracknell, I said I had lost my parents.
It would be nearer the truth to say that my parents
seem to have lost me... I don't actually know who I am
by birth. I was...well found.

PORTRAIT #3. Found?

JAX. The late dear Thomas Cardew, a wise and wonderful person with a very charitable disposition, found me, and gave me the name of Worthing, because they happened to have a first-class ticket to Worthing in their pocket at the time. Worthing is a place in Sussex. It is a seaside resort.

LADY BRACKNELL. And just where did this charitable ticket-holder find you?

JAX. In a handbag.

PORTRAIT #1. A handbag?

PORTRAIT #3. A handbag!

(**LADY BRACKNELL** *rises in disgust.*)

LADY BRACKNELL. *A handbag!?!*

(**PORTRAIT #2** *faints in disbelief.*)

JAX. Yes, Lady Bracknell. I was in a handbag – a somewhat large, black leather handbag with handles on it – an ordinary handbag –

LADY BRACKNELL. In what locality was this "ordinary handbag" to be found?

JAX. At the cloak room of Victoria Station.

(*The* **PORTRAITS** *all sigh in disbelief.*)

(*With a flourish,* **LADY BRACKNELL** *closes their book.*)

LADY BRACKNELL. Thus my choice is made for me. Ernest Worthing, how could you imagine that I would ever allow my dearest Gwyn to be joined in matrimony to nothing more than a parcel. You have no family, a name of convenience, why one doesn't even know if you're British.

JAX. I assure you, I am.

LADY BRACKNELL. So you say…

> YOUR RATTY BAG
> IS YOUR OWN BUS'NESS
> RICHES TO RAGS
> WILL NOT BUY KISSES
> THOUGH TO BE FAIR,
> I'M MOVED BY YOUR HEARTFELT BID…

PORTRAITS.
> BUT HEAVEN FORBID!

LADY BRACKNELL.
> NOT BORN WITH IT.

PORTRAITS.
> BREAKIN' IT DOWN!

LADY BRACKNELL.
> NOT BORN WITH IT.

PORTRAITS.
> GET OUT OF TOWN!

LADY BRACKNELL.
> I'M BORN WITH IT!

JAX. But Lady Bracknell, please.

LADY BRACKNELL.	**PORTRAITS.**

I GOT MY
   GRANDMOTHER'S NOSE
FOR THE STENCH OF
   THE CLIMB.
	SHE'S GOT HER
	   GRANDMOTHER'S NOSE
	FOR THE STENCH OF
	   THE CLIMB.

LADY BRACKNELL.
> YOU GOT A –

Actually, could you just come a bit closer – well. Hm. Interesting. Yes…

> YOU GOT A NOBODY NOSE!

PORTRAITS.

NOBODY NOSE!

LADY BRACKNELL.

NOBODY KNOWS

> (**LADY BRACKNELL** *and the* **PORTRAITS** *begin to exit.*)

PORTRAITS.

MAYBE SHE'S,

MAYBE SHE'S,

MAYBE SHE'S,

MAYBE SHE'S,

LADY BRACKNELL.

BORN WITH IT.

> (**LADY BRACKNELL** *and* **PORTRAITS** *exit.*)

> (**JAX** *stands alone for a moment – overwhelmed.*)

Scene Six

> (**ALGY** *enters.*)

ALGY. It didn't go off well, did it? Well no matter, we can comfort ourselves with a lovely dinner at Dorian's.

JAX. Your Aunt Augusta is perfectly unbearable. I'm sorry Algy, I shouldn't be talking about your relations that way.

ALGY. Oh, please continue. There's nothing I love more than hearing my relations abused. It is the only thing that allows me to put up with them at all.

> (**ALGY** *is aiming the comment at the* **PORTRAITS**, *which are now all gone.*)

Where have all my pictures gone?

JAX. Without my darling Gwyn, what shall I do? I am their Ernest.

WILDES. Ernest!

JAX. Thank you. I needed that.

ALGY. And did you tell Gwyn about your being their Ernest in town but Cecile's Jax in the country?

JAX. My dear fellow, the truth isn't quite the sort of thing one tells to a nice, sweet, person such as Gwyn...

> (**GWYN** *rushes back into the room.*)

Gwyn! Here you are! Again! Isn't that wonderful, Algy?

GWYN. Algy, kindly turn your back. I have something very particular to say to Ernest.

> (**ALGY** *turns.*)

Ernest, my love, from the expression on Mamma's face, I fear we shall never be married.

ALGY. I've seen that face.

GWYN. Algy, Turn Around. *(Then.)* Although she may prevent us from marrying, and I may be forced to marry someone else, nothing can ever alter my eternal devotion to you. When Mamma related to me the story of your rather romantic origin in the handbag.

JAX. I assure you, it was a very nice handbag.

GWYN. I've no doubt, dearest one. I swear to you, that no matter what, you will always be my one and only Ernest!

WILDES. Ernest!

JAX. Oh, my love, my Gwyn. We must be married.

    *(**JAX** moves towards **GWYN**.)*

GWYN. Please, not in front of Algy! I have your address in town, but what is your address in the country?

JAX. The Manor house. Woolton, Hertfordshire.

    *(Both **ALGY** and **GWYN** write this down.)*

GWYN. I shall write to you. But if we truly want to be together, it may be necessary to do something desperate.

    *(**ALGY** turns around and pushes **GWYN** out of the room.)*

ALGY. Before all this desperation, we have reservations.

    *(**JAX** takes **GWYN**'s arm, and walks them to the door.)*

JAX. Let me see you in your carriage, my dearest darling. My Gwyn.

GWYN. You may, my Ernest.

    (They exit.)

ALGY. My stomach.

> (**WILLS** *enters.*)

WILLS. May I remove the tray?

ALGY. What? Oh of course, and have Wince pack my bags. I'm off to the country. Poor Bunbury is ill again.

> (**WILLS** *sneezes.*)

Scene Seven

[MUSIC NO. 05A – BECOME YOURSELF (REPRISE)]

ALGY. See, you're catching on already.

CUE THE COUNTRYSIDE,
CUE THE FLOWER CROWNS
CUE THE BAREST FEET
AND ORGANZA GOWNS.

(**ALGY** *exits.*)

(**WINCE** *enters now dressed in pastel country attire. We have travled to the picturesque English Countryside of the Romantics, filled with flowers and frolic. The old* **WINCE** *is only betrayed by the clipboard.*)

WINCE.

OH, OH

WILDES.

WHERE THE SHEEP ARE LOUD,

WILDE SOLO 1.

BAHHH

WILDES.

AND THE BEES ARE BLESSED.

WILDE SOLO 2.

BUZZZZ

WILDES.

WHERE THE FARMERS WORK,

WILDE SOLO 3.

HOE!

WILDES.
AND THE WEALTHY REST.

WINCE. And so, as if by magic...

(**SLOUCH** *enters, in clothes even more in the spirit of spring, with a basket of flower petals that they sprinkle on the ground!*)

SLOUCH. *(With a big flourish of flowers.)* Abra-ca-dabra!

WINCE. *(To **SLOUCH**.)* Theatrical magic needn't be so loud, THANK YOU.

*(The **WILDES** create a pastoral extravaganza.)*

WILDES.
BECOME THE FIELDS OF ALBION.
BECOME THE HILLS OF GREAT BRITA'N.
THE LEAPING SLEEPING FOWL AND FAWN
BECOME –

*(The **WILDES** create the pastoral English countryside.)*

WINCE. *(To audience.)* We are transported to the glory of the English countryside –

WILDES.
BECOME –

WINCE. Here, the young and innocent Cecile is looked after by their companion and tutor...

WILDES.
BECOME –

(They all wait a beat.)

WINCE. Where is Cecile? And where is Prism?

OSCAR. Cecile fired Prism. They left.

WINCE. This will not do at all. Slouch!

SLOUCH. *(Reentering.)* I'm not supposed to be in this scene, am I?

WINCE. *(To* **SLOUCH.***)* No, but you are now. Now, you're Prism.

SLOUCH. But I can't act. I don't even know the lines.

WINCE. You'll read them.

> **(WINCE** *picks up a book from the table and hands it to* **SLOUCH.***)*

There you are. Everything you need to know is there in that book. And as for the rest.

> **(WINCE** *claps and calls to the wings.)*

Bring on the Prism costume, please.

> **(WINCE** *calls on some* **WILDES,** *who bring a script, a costume piece, and a grey wig. Prism is a much older person of another gender, in very dowdy and greyish clothes.)*

I don't see how some people think they have the right to alter the course of the play like that. We need a Prism. They're integral to the plot.

> *(The* **WILDES** *reveal a transformed* **SLOUCH,** *as Prism, who holds the script.* **SLOUCH** *should read their lines as Prism from the script throughout the scene.)*

Yes. That will do.

SLOUCH. But what's my motivation?

WINCE. To continue the play! Thank you.

> **(WINCE** *forces* **SLOUCH** *in their seat and attempts to restart the scene. Lines in quotations are lines* **SLOUCH** *speaks as Prism.)*

WINCE. And so the young and headstrong Cecile Cardew sits enjoying their studies with their sad,

(**SLOUCH** *becomes sad.*)

SLOUCH. "Boo-hoo-hoo-hoo"

WINCE. Old.

(**SLOUCH** *becomes old.*)

SLOUCH. "Everything hurts and I hate young people's music."

WINCE. Spinster and Tutor, Prism.

(**WINCE** *moves away from the scene.*)

SLOUCH. *(Calling to **WINCE**.)* Is that like Scottish?

[MUSIC NO. 06 – OUT HERE]

*(Not getting an answer, **SLOUCH** shrugs and goes back to their seat to play Prism)*

WINCE. To the heart of Hertfordshire where the impressionable young Cecile Cardew...

(A flourish.)

Is probably off with their confounded diary!

(**WINCE** *exits.*)

(**CECILE** *rushes onstage, writing furiously in their diary.*)

CECILE.
RUN OUT TO THE WILDS OF THESE UNCHARTED WOODS,
OUT WHERE YOU CAN HIDE FROM THESE UNHOLY RULES.
BRAND SPANKING NEW, BABE,
BREATHE IN THAT COLD AIR.
HEAD TO THE FOREST,
SEE WHAT YOU FIND THERE.

(Writing in their diary.)

"And then I felt that familiar bubbling feeling, that effervescence of emotion, that pops out of me, and must find its way to you, dear diary, since nowhere else, can I share such private and personal thoughts. I wonder if there could be, somehow, someday, someone. Someone brave, and strong and courageous, like dear cousin Ernest, though we have never met, who I could speak to as freely as write here."

WRITING DOWN THE CERTAIN TRUTH THAT SPINS FROM
　　LIES.
SCRIBBLE DOWN THE WORDS MOST SURE TO SCANDALIZE.
DARE LIKE A DEVIL
AND MAKE AN ART OF IT.
SHOOT LIKE AN ARROW
STRAIGHT TO THE HEART OF IT.

WRITE IT ALL DOWN
SO YOU NEVER FORGET,
NEVER FORGET. MM
WRITE IT ALL DOWN
SO YOU NEVER FORGET,
NEVER FORGET.
LIFE COULD START RIGHT NOW.

OUT HERE, OUT HERE, OUT HERE
THE FIELDS ARE ENDLESS,
THE TREES ARE ENDLESS.
OUT HERE, OUT HERE, OUT HERE
YOU'RE RUNNING BREATHLESS,
EVER-RESTLESS
PRAYING THAT SOMETHING WILL APPEAR.
IS ANYONE ELSE OUT HERE?

SLOUCH. "Oh there you are! Now sit down for your studies like a good ward."

(Trying to do a truly terrible Scottish accent.) "Your German grammar is on the table."

CECILE. But I don't like German. It isn't a becoming language at all. I know perfectly well that I look quite plain after my German lesson.

SLOUCH. Then I say...

(Reading lines again.) "But you don't want to disappoint your guardian, Jax. They will be so pleased to hear you can Sprachen the Duetsche."

CECILE.

    BREAK OUT FROM THE TIES THAT BIND BEHIND FOUR
       WALLS

SLOUCH. Oh, you're going to sing again. Alright.

CECILE.

    FREEING UP THE MIND THAT WINDS IN SUDDEN SQUALLS.
    SHINE LIKE YOU'RE BURNING
    TO LIGHT A BONFIRE.
    CHASING A VISION
    THAT SETS YOUR SIGHTS HIGHER.
    WRITE IT ALL DOWN
    SO YOU NEVER FORGET,
    NEVER FORGET.
    WRITE IT ALL DOWN
    SO YOU NEVER FORGET,
    NEVER FORGET.
    SECURE YOUR FATE RIGHT NOW.

    OUT HERE, OUT HERE, OUT HERE
    THE WORDS ARE ENDLESS,
    THE PAGES ENDLESS.
    OUT HERE, OUT HERE, OUT HERE
    YOU'RE RUNNING BREATHLESS,
    EVER-RESTLESS
    PRAYING THAT SOMETHING WILL APPEAR.
    IS ANYONE ELSE OUT HERE?
    READY, SET, GO
    DONE WITH DAYDREAMING.

READY TO KNOW
WHO CAN HEAR ME SCREAMING.
OUT HERE, OUT HERE, OUT HERE

(Sincere, lost.)

THE HOURS ARE ENDLESS.
THE DAYS ARE ENDLESS
OUT HERE, OUT HERE, OUT HERE

(Gathering her energy back up.)

I'M RUNNING BREATHLESS
EVER-RESTLESS
WONDERS NEVER CEASE.
DAYDREAMS CAN APPEAR.
SOMETHING WILL RELEASE.
THIS WILL BE MY YEAR.
LIFE WILL FIND ME WAY OUT HERE.

*(***SLOUCH*** can't help themself and joins in the applause for ***CECILE***.)*

SLOUCH. *(Applauding.)* Oh you're very good.

CECILE. Oh, how I wish dear Jax would allow that unfortunate sibling of theirs, with that marvelous name...

*(The ***WILDES*** pop out again.)*

WILDES. Ernest.

SLOUCH. Oh, we do that here too?

WILDES. Yes.

CECILE. Yes, Ernest. If only Jax would allow Ernest to come visit us sometimes, I'm sure we could prevail upon them to leave their wicked ways behind them once and for all.

SLOUCH. Then I say, "I doubt there's much reforming of a character so 'irretrievably weak and vacillating' as Ernest."

(The **WILDES** *pop in again.)*

WILDES. Ernest.

SLOUCH. "Besides, I am not in favor of this modern mania for turning bad people into good people at a moment's notice. Let people be as they are."

*(***O'FLAHERTIE*** enters with a note. ***CECILE****'s reverie pops like a soap bubble.)*

CECILE. What is it, O'Flahertie?

O'FLAHERTIE. There's a note here for...

SLOUCH. *(Scanning the script.)* No, no, no, that's not right.

O'FLAHERTIE. *(Stops.)* What?

SLOUCH. *(Trying to whisper.)* In the script. It says, "Suddenly the dirty old gardener Merriman, approaches with a card."

O'FLAHERTIE. It doesn't say that.

*(***WINCE*** enters carrying a hat, a grey beard, and a rake.)*

WINCE. It does. Very good, Slouch. *(Then, to* **O'FLAHERTIE.***)* Come along, O'Flahertie. You're Merriman, now.

*(***WINCE*** dresses ***O'FLAHERTIE*** as Merriman.)*

SLOUCH. Then I say...

(Doing accent again.) "Now that we've finished with our German..."

(Stopping.) Can I stop doing the accent?

CECILE. I wish you would.

SLOUCH. Alright.

(*Back into scene.*) "Now that we've finished with our German, shall we move on to something truly exciting like Politics or Algebra?"

CECILE.   Politics are nothing but Algebra. They both promise equilibrium without any practical way of getting there.

SLOUCH.   Oh, that's very smart.

(**O'FLAHERTIE** *is now Merriman. Merriman has a dirty face and mustache, a wobbling gait, and perhaps a distinct voice.*)

O'FLAHERTIE.   (*As Merriman.*) Pardon, but there's an Ernest Worthing at the door.

CECILE.   My guardian's sibling whom I have never met?! How thrilling!

(**CECILE** *starts to write in her diary.*)

SLOUCH.   Then I say...

CECILE.   Just say it.

SLOUCH.   "Ernest Worthing! The devil incarnate! Did you tell this Worthing that the other Worthing is away in town?"

O'FLAHERTIE.   (*As Merriman.*) I did and much to their credit, they seemed rather disappointed. However, when I mentioned that you and Cecile were here in the garden, their former sorrow lifted into bleats of joy.

CECILE.   (*Copying into their diary.*) ...were here in the garden. Was it bleats of joy?

O'FLAHERTIE.   (*As Merriman.*) Yes. Bleats like sheep. They said they were most anxious to speak with you privately.

CECILE.   Me!

SLOUCH. "Oh, I don't know…"

CECILE. I do!

> (*To* **O'FLAHERTIE** a*s Merriman.*) Please ask this wicked Worthing to come here. You've done very well, Merriman.

O'FLAHERTIE. (*Breaking character.*) I have, haven't I?

> (**O'FLAHERTIE** *spits their tongue out at* **SLOUCH** *and leaves.*)

CECILE. How do I look? I've never met anyone as wicked as Ernest Worthing.

WILDES. Ernest!

SLOUCH. "Cecile, dear, I don't know if it's altogether proper for someone so young to be left alone with someone reportedly uncivilized and dangerous as Ernest Worthing."

WILDES. Ernest!

> (*Enter* **ALGY** *as Ernest.*)

ALGY. That's me. Here I am.

Scene Eight

[MUSIC NO. 6B – BECOME ERNEST]

(**CECILE**, *alone, prepares themself to look alluring for their very dastardly cousin.* **ALGY** *enters looking "very interesting," with an eye patch.*)

ALGY.
BECOME, BECOME, BECOME A ROGUE.
SO SCANDALOUS AND SO EN VOGUE.
NOW I FOR ONE
WILL HAVE SOME FUN.
BECOME, BECOME, BECOME…
ERNEST!

SLOUCH. Oh, they do look like a baddie, don't they?

CECILE. *(Suddenly frantic.)* Get out now or I'll steal your book!

(**SLOUCH** *hurries offstage, clutching their script.*)

ALGY. You must be my little cousin, Cecile.

CECILE. You are under some strange mistake, I am not little.

(Standing up from their chair.) In fact, I believe I am more than usually tall for my age.

(**CECILE** *moves closer to* **ALGY**.)

But, yes, I am your cousin Cecile, in that you are my guardian Jax's wicked sibling.

ALGY. Cecile, you mustn't believe me to be truly wicked.

CECILE. Oh but I want to! All this time, I've heard nothing but tales of your scandalous nature. It would be almost demoralizing to think you'd just been pretending to be wicked, while being really good all along.

ALGY. Well... I have been rather...reckless.

CECILE. That's precisely what Jax has told me. It's a good thing they aren't here to greet you. I imagine they'd be somewhat perturbed that you're not on the boat to Australia.

ALGY. To...where?

CECILE. Yes, Jax told me that they were going up to town to help with all the emigration papers, and to see that you've had your shots for your departure to Australia...

ALGY. I'm afraid to say, dear Cecile, your dear guardian Jax has deceived you.

CECILE. That doesn't sound like Jax. They said at dinner on Wednesday night –

(*Reading from diary.*) – that they'd finally given you an ultimatum, that you must choose between this world, the next world, or Australia.

ALGY. And I chose Australia?! I can assure you that if I had any choice whatsoever, I would always choose this world, for you are in this world.

CECILE. You mustn't be naughty, just because we're alone.

ALGY. Oh, are we? I hadn't noticed. I promise, I shall be on my best behaviour, and if I stray even the teensiest bit, I give you full permission to correct me.

CECILE. Me? Why, what would I know of correction? Especially for someone as hardened and degenerate as yourself?

ALGY. I'm sure you could find some instruction in one of your books.

(**ALGY** *accidentally picks up Cecile's diary and starts to open it.*)

CECILE. *(Suddenly scary.)* Put That Down!

(**ALGY** *slowly puts the diary down.*)

I'm sorry, it's my diary.

ALGY. I've always found that only the most scandalous people keep diaries.

CECILE. I keep a diary in order to enter all the wonderful secrets of my life. If I didn't write them down, I should probably forget all about them.

ALGY. *(They move closer.)* I hope Cecile, I shall not offend you if I state quite frankly and openly that you seem to me to be in every way the visible personification of absolute perfection.

CECILE. I feel very similarly about you. I have noted it several times in my diary.

ALGY. Just from this first meeting?

CECILE. Heavens no, I have dreamed of you for years.

[MUSIC NO. 07 – WILD]

Wicked Ernest. Scandalous Ernest. Truly beastly Ernest!

ALGY. How strange, that having just met, we know each other so well.

CECILE.
IF I SAY I NEED A VILLAIN FOR MY LATEST PASSION PLAY.

ALGY.
IF I SAY I'LL NEED A TWIRLY MOUSTACHE AND AN ATTACHÉ

CECILE.
IF I SAY I'M DOWN FOR THAT –

ALGY.
I'LL MEET YOUR DREAMS HALFWAY.

CECILE.
WILL YOU GO WILD

ALGY.

WILD?

CECILE.

WILD WITH ME?

ALGY.

IF I SAY A SUDDEN BIT OF SCANDAL LEAVES ME
    INDISPOSED –

CECILE.

THEN I SAY A LITTLE BIT OF DRAMA KEEPS US ON OUR
    TOES –

ALGY.

IF I SWEAR TO SPEAK IN COUPLETS

CECILE.

DARLING, I'LL PROPOSE.

ALGY.

THEN I'LL GO WILD

CECILE.

WILD,

ALGY & CECILE.

WILD

CECILE.

FOR YOU.

FOLLOW MY LEAD

ALGY.

YOU FOLLOW MINE

CECILE.

MAKE A BIG SCENE.

ALGY.

FEED ME MY LINE.

ALGY & CECILE.

AND WHERE IT ENDS

NO ONE CAN SAY

ALGY.

BUT I'LL CHOOSE YOU EVERY DAY.

CECILE.

IF I SAY I'M HOT TO TANGO, WILL YOU GLIDE ME 'CROSS
THE FLOOR?

ALGY.

IF I SAY THE THRILL IS IN THE CHASE, WILL YOU RUN FOR
THE DOOR?

CECILE.

IF I SAY I CRAVE ADVENTURE –

ALGY.

SIGN ME UP FOR MORE
OF GOING WILD.

CECILE.

WILD

ALGY & CECILE.

WILD
WITH YOU.

ALGY. This is all moving so quickly.

CECILE. Oh, I don't think so considering we've been
engaged since last February –

ALGY. We have? But we've only just met today.

CECILE. Yes, in life. But in my diary, we have been engaged
for months.

ALGY. You're a little kooky, aren't you?

CECILE. Li'l bit.

(They dance.)

ALGY & CECILE.

IF I SAY I NEVER KNEW ANOTHER SOUL WOULD SEE MY
CHARMS.

CECILE.

IF I SAY I'LL ALWAYS ASK CONSENT 'CAUSE ASKING NEVER HARMS.

ALGY.

IF YOU SAY YOU'D LIKE TO HOLD ME,

ALGY & CECILE.

I'LL FALL IN YOUR ARMS

(They look at each other for consent. After a moment, they enthusiastically embrace.)

ALGY.

THAT WOULD BE WILD

CECILE.

WILD

ALGY & CECILE.

WILD

CECILE.

IT'S TRUE.

*(**ALGY** stands on one of the chairs, putting their right leg on the back, and riding it to the floor.)*

ALGY.

STILL WE BEGIN

*(**CECILE** repeats the gesture.)*

CECILE.

ON WITH THE DANCE,

(They each go to another chair and repeat the gesture.)

ALGY & CECILE.

DON'T CALL IT LOVE

DON'T CALL IT ROMANCE

CALL IT

WILD

> *(They end up embracing in the center, all the chairs laid out. The moment which has been adventurous and grand, suddenly becomes intimate and close.)*

ALGY.

WILD

CECILE.

WILD

ALGY & CECILE.

ME AND YOU.

> *(***ALGY***, feeling the moment, goes in for a kiss, but* ***CECILE*** *stops them.)*

CECILE. Before we proceed, I feel as though I must make a confession to you, dear Ernest.

ALGY. Yes, me Ernest. Whatever can it be, my sweet darling Cecile?

CECILE. You mustn't laugh at me, darling, but it had always been a childish dream of mine to love someone named Ernest.

WILDES. Ernest.

ALGY. Oh no, not you too?

CECILE. There is something in that name that inspires absolute confidence. I pity the poor dab whose spouse is not called Ernest.

WILDES. Ernest.

ALGY. But my dear Cecile, do you mean to say you could not love me if my name was something like...oh I don't know...Algy?

CECILE. Algae...like pond scum?

ALGY. Well that's perhaps not the first thing I would think of...

CECILE. I might respect an Algy, I might even admire their character, but I fear that I could never give them my undivided attention. And I could certainly never marry an Algy.

ALGY. Never?

CECILE. Never. Never. Never.

ALGY. I must be christened... I mean we must be married at once!

(**ALGY** *gets up.*)

CECILE. Ernest, my love, where are you going?

ALGY. I must away, but I shall be back before you can say, Ernest Worthing. And have it mean me!

(**ALGY** *dashes off.* **O'FLAHERTIE** *enters as Merriman again.*)

O'FLAHERTIE. (*As Merriman.*) Beggin' your pardon, Cecile...

CECILE. You can take that off, O'Flahertie.

O'FLAHERTIE. I'm actually kind of liking it. (*Then as Merriman.*) A Gwyn Fairfax has just arrived looking for Ernest Worthing.

CECILE. They've only just left. Well, you must bring this Gwyn Fairfax to me. And we must have tea.

O'FLAHERTIE. *Tea?*

[MUSIC NO. 07A – WILD TAG]

CECILE. Tea, Merriman. In the Garden.

(*As* **O'FLAHERTIE** *exits.*)

IT'S GETTING
WILD, WILD, WILD
OUT HERE.

    (**CECILE** *exits.*)

Scene Nine

(**JAX** *enters wearing mourning clothes, and putting on a show of misery.*)

JAX. *(Really playing the melodrama.)* Oh Ernest! Why did you have to die! My poor Ernest! Gone too soon! Gone... Gone...

(Looking around for everyone.) Gone? Where is everyone?

(**SLOUCH** *enters with their script.*)

Oh, Slouch. There you are. Where is everyone else?

SLOUCH. Oh, I'm Prism now. The dowdy companion and tutor of young Cecile Cardew. See it says so in my book.

JAX. Oh, alright then. Well, it also says you should be surprised to see me.

SLOUCH. Does it? It does!

(**SLOUCH** *looks back into the script, suddenly surprised.*)

"Jax Worthing! This is indeed a surprise. We were not expecting you till Monday afternoon. I trust that this garb of woe does not portend some terrible calamity?"

JAX. I'm afraid you are correct, dear Prism. Someone has died. Someone very dear.

SLOUCH. "Who?"

JAX. My sibling. My poor Ernest, I'm afraid. Poor Ernest is no more.

SLOUCH. *(Confused, breaking character.)* From the last scene? But how did they die?

JAX. They were in Paris. At some dreadful little boîte, where the lowest of the low consort with artists and bon vivants of all types. They apparently attempted the new dance-craze of the Can-Can, only to find they couldn't-couldn't. Poor sad Ernest. Gone too soon. R.I.P. Kaput-ski. Dead.

SLOUCH. Well, that is sad. They seemed so well just a moment ago.

JAX. Even the loss of a, shall we say troublesome, sibling, is still a very great loss indeed! That is why I must have a vicar.

SLOUCH. I have an Oscar, a Fingal, an O'Flahertie, a Wills...

JAX. A reverend. Clergy of some sort. *(Calling off.)* Wince!

*(***WINCE*** enters.)*

WINCE. Jax Worthing, what a surprise! I trust this garb of woe does not portend...

SLOUCH. We did that bit already.

JAX. Wince, I am in need of a vicar. My sibling has died, and I would like to be christened.

WINCE. That seems a strange sequence of sacraments. Your sibling was just asking for the same.

JAX. My what now was how?

*(***ALGY*** enters eating lunch.)*

ALGY. Jax, it is I, Ernest! I've come home!

JAX. You have not! You're dead.

SLOUCH. It's a miracle!

WINCE. Slouch! Enough! Come with me!

*(***SLOUCH*** and ***WINCE*** exit.)*

JAX. Algy, what are you doing here?

[MUSIC NO. 7B – THE SOCIALS TODAY (REPRISE)]

ALGY.

> I'M YOUR SIBLING WHO'S BEEN REFORMED!
> MET YOUR WARD.
> GOT ENGAGED.
> THAT WAS GREAT.

JAX.

> YOU'RE A FRAUD.

ALGY.

> WELL, THAT'S ODD –
> DO YOU THINK IT'S A FAM'LY TRAIT?
> JUST ADMIT
> WE'RE THE SAME.

JAX.

> WE ARE NOT.

ALGY.

> IT'S A GAME.

JAX.

> IT'S A PLOT.

ALGY.

> LIKE THE PLOT OF A COSTUME DRAMA?

JAX. Algy, you must leave at once. If Cecile were to see you...

ALGY. They would fall hopelessly in love? We've done that bit. We're engaged to be married in fact!

JAX. You're nothing of the kind. Merriman?

(**O'FLAHERTIE** enters as Merriman again.)

O'FLAHERTIE. Yes, that's still me. What can I do for you?

JAX. Where is my ward, Cecile Cardew now?

O'FLAHERTIE. In the garden with Gwyn Fairfax.

ALGY & JAX.
WITH WHO?

O'FLAHERTIE. Yes, they're about to have tea. It's a very
dignified thing to do.

(**O'FLAHERTIE** *exits.*)

ALGY.
AND NOW THE PLOT IS TWISTING.

JAX.
SO I NEED A PROPER COVER.

ALGY.
ALL OF US ARE TRYSTING.

JAX.
IT'S A SCANDAL!

ALGY.
CALL YOUR SECRET LOVER!

WILDES.
THROW YOUR HANDS UP,
THE WORLD'LL HANG ON

ALGY.
CAN'T KEEP UP WITH THE SOCIALS

JAX. This is very very bad.

WILDES.
BENDING THE RULES
IN GAMES THAT WE PLAY.

ALGY. They're just having tea, Jax. What could go wrong?

ALGY & WILDES.
CAN'T KEEP UP WITH THE SOCIALS
HEY, HEY,
UH-UH-UH-OH,

(**WINCE** *and* **SLOUCH**, *carrying their script, enter.*)

SLOUCH. Well, they're in a fine pickle.

ALGY & WILDES.

UH-UH-UH-OH,

SLOUCH. I've been reading ahead.

WILDES.

CAN'T KEEP UP!

WINCE. But our audience has not, Slouch.

WILDES.

CAN'T KEEP UP!

WINCE. Gentles all, with this we conclude Act One.

WINCE.	**ALL (EXCEPT WINCE).**
Feel free to stretch your legs, discuss the brilliance of Wilde, or perhaps enjoy a baked good of some sort, while we prepare for Act Two.	CAN'T KEEP UP – CAN'T KEEP UP – CAN'T KEEP – CAN'T KEEP UP – CAN'T KEEP UP – CAN'T KEEP – CAN'T KEEP UP – CAN'T KEEP UP – CAN'T KEEP –

ALGY & WILDES.

CAN'T KEEP UP!

ALGY.

WITH THE SOCIALS

WILDES.

OH

CAN'T KEEP UP!

SLOUCH. There are baked goods? I knew I liked the Theater!

ALL.
TODAY!

ALGY.
OH-OH-OH-OH!

WILDES.
HEY!

End of Act I

ACT II

Scene Ten

(**WINCE** *enters with the* **WILDES**, *followed by* **SLOUCH**, *still dressed at Prism.*)

WINCE. And now, we come to the main event. Wildes! To your stations!

[MUSIC NO. 08 – TEA FIGHT]

(*The* **WILDES** *begin to set the space for the tea.*)

SLOUCH. What's happening? I haven't read this bit yet.

WINCE. Welcome, gentles all, to the crowning achievement of a civil and polite society. The High English Tea.

(*The* **WILDES** *dance into the space, creating the atmosphere for a High English Tea. A small table, chairs, tea, adornments, and refreshments. There is a heightened tone of grave civility.*)

The Height of grace, The triumph of style,

The cream of society linger awhile

Over pots of hot tea,

we come to this epitome

WINCE. of dignity and decorum

Where our two loves may find a forum...

SLOUCH. *(Having read ahead.)* Oh wait, they're having tea together, but they both think they're in love with…

WINCE. Enough, Slouch. This is all a comedic farce, and one of its hallmarks is mistaken identities.

SLOUCH. But we all know who they are.

WINCE. Yes, but they don't. And that's half the fun.

> *(Barreling through.)*

The hallmark of the English Tea

Is style, grace and civility.

And with these contenders,

We find no offenders

Of anything uncouth…

SLOUCH. *(Aside.)* Or anyone knowing the truth.

WINCE. This is a High English Tea.

SLOUCH. Sounds like a fight to me!

> *(The **WILDES** respond physically, and they form pairs of fighting opponents. The beat drops.)*

WILDES.

TEA FIGHT! TEA FIGHT!
HMM.
TEA FIGHT! TEA FIGHT!
HMM.

WINCE. No, no, NO! You have all taken liberties enough! This is the pinnacle of comedic style from our dear Oscar Wilde. And that is why we're here, isn't it? Isn't it?

> *(The **WILDES** reluctantly agree with sound. **WINCE** takes control of the story – nodding for **CECILE** to enter with the utmost gentility.)*

COMPOSE YOURSELVES AS
I PRESENT AT ONCE
M. CECILE CARDEW,
SUCH AN ENGLISH ROSE.

(**CECILE** *curtsies or bows. Whatever is natural to them in a genteel setting.*)

SLOUCH. *(Aside.)*
JUST AS THORNY.

(**GWYN FAIRFAX** *enters from the opposite side of the stage.*)

WINCE.
HERE, WE HAVE THE MILD
GWYN FAIRFAX

SLOUCH.
WILL IT COME EVER TO BLOWS?

WINCE. *(Aside.)*
DON'T BE ORN'RY.

(**WINCE** *and* **SLOUCH** *and the other* **WILDES** *witness high tea as servants.*)

GWYN.
MAY I CALL YOU CECILE?

CECILE.
YES, MAY I CALL YOU GWYN?

WILDES.
MM-MM-MM

WINCE.
THIS IS GOING SWIMMINGLY.

SLOUCH.
BUT NEITHER WILL WIN.

WILDES.

MM-MM-MM

GWYN. You are here on a visit, one imagines.

CECILE. Oh, no, I live here.

GWYN. With your mother or some other relative of advanced years, one hopes?

CECILE. Well, there is Prism, my tutor, but it's mostly just myself and my dear guardian Worthing.

GWYN. *What?*

CECILE.

I'M DEAR WORTHING'S WARD.

GWYN.

I WILL EAT MY HAT.

SLOUCH.

CECILE SCORED ONE FOR THAT

SLOUCH & WILDES.

THAT THAT

THAT'S THE TEA.

WILDES.

THAT'S THE TEA

THAT'S A HOT

POT OF TEA

LET IT SPILL

WHERE IT WILL.

HIGH VOICES.

WE GOTTA

TEA FIGHT

OSCAR.

SUBTLE DOUBT

AND THEY CRACK.

WILLS & SPERANZA.

FIRST THEY POUT

THEN ATTACK.

WILDES.

COME ON AND
TEA FIGHT! TEA FIGHT!
HMM.
TEA FIGHT! TEA FIGHT!
HMM.

WINCE. You're goading them into something untoward. These are cultured and dignified young people, who would never resort to any sort of fisticuffs. Isn't that right?

CECILE.	**GWYN.**
No! Never!	The thought never entered my mind.

(High tea.)

WINCE. Then shall I pour?

(CECILE *nods and* **WINCE** *pours.)*

GWYN. So dear Ernest is your guardian. I can't imagine why they didn't mention that. Or you...

CECILE. I beg your pardon, but did you say Ernest? Oh, but it is not *Ernest* Worthing who is my guardian.

GWYN. Oh, that is a relief.

CECILE. Ernest Worthing is my fiancée!

WILDES. Ernest.

(SLOUCH *and the* **WILDES** *react.)*

GWYN.

MY DEAREST CECILE,
YOU MAKE SOME MISTAKE

GWYN.

FOR ERNEST WORTHING
IS ENGAGED TO ME.

> (**WINCE** *tries to keep both of them from blowing their tops.*)

WINCE.
KINDLY STAY SEATED.

CECILE.
I'M AFRAID YOU'RE WRONG,
M. FAIRFAX,
FOR I AM THEIR SPOUSE TO BE.

SLOUCH.
IT'S GETTING HEATED!

> (**WINCE** *shushes* **SLOUCH.**)

GWYN.
THAT IS VERY CURIOUS.

CECILE.
MY JOURNAL CONFIRMS.

> (**CECILE** *pulls out their diary.*)

WILDES.
HMM.

GWYN.
I *TOO* KEEP A JOURNAL.

> (**GWYN** *pulls out their diary. Both point to the facts.*)

GWYN & CECILE.
THERE! IN *BLACK AND WHITE* TERMS!

> (*They exchange diaries and each examines the other's diary.*)

WILDES.
HMM!

(They throw the diaries across the stage. **WINCE** *attempts to collect them and keep the table from rattling.)*

GWYN.

I HAVE PRIOR CLAIM!

CECILE.

DARLING, DON'T GET SHRILL!

WINCE.

KEEP IT TAME OR YOU'LL

WINCE & WILDES.

SPILL! SPILL!

SPILL THE TEA

WILDES.

THAT'S THE TEA

SLOUCH.

THAT COULD SCALD.

THIRD DEGREE.

WILDES.

LET IT SPILL

WHERE IT WILL.

HIGH VOICES.

WE GOTTA

TEA FIGHT

O'FLAHERTIE.

HAIR'S UNCOIFFED.

WILDE.

WE ARE RAPT.

OSCAR.

GLOVES ARE OFF.

OSCAR, O'FLAHERTIE & WILDE.

NERVES HAVE SNAPPED.

WILDES.
> COME ON AND
> TEA FIGHT! TEA FIGHT!

WINCE. More tea?

GWYN. Yes. Please.

WILDES.
> TEA FIGHT! TEA FIGHT!

CECILE. Sugar?

GWYN. Sugar is not fashionable any longer. Perhaps, if you lived in town you would know that.

> (**CECILE** *puts a fistful of sugar in* **GWYN**'s *tea.*)

WILDES.
> HMM

CECILE. Some cake?

GWYN. Bread and butter. Cake is rarely seen at the best houses in town.

CECILE. No cake and no manners, I must write that down.
> I WAS NOT RAISED IN A GUTTER.

GWYN.
> CAKE MAKES MY WHOLE BODY SHUDDER.

CECILE.
> SINCE YOU *SO* LOVE BREAD AND BUTTER!

> (**CECILE** *takes some bread and butter and squashes it into* **GWYN**'s *face.*)

WINCE. Oh dear. This has gotten intensely out of hand.

GWYN.
> SINCE CAKE SETS YOUR HEART AFLUTTER!

(**GWYN** *pushes cake into* **CECILE**'s *face.*

(They both take some of the other tea accoutrement and start circling each other. One with the sugar bowl, throwing cubes. One with tea splashing.)

WILDES.

HMM-YA!
THAT'S THE TEA!
THAT'S THE TEA!
THAT'S AS HOT
AS CAN BE.
LET IT SPILL
WHERE IT WILL.

CECILE & GWYN.

WE GOT
A

CECILE, GWYN & WILDES.

TEA FIGHT

CECILE & GWYN.

NOW!

WILDES.

THAT'S THE TEA.
THAT'S THE TEA
THAT'S AS HOT
AS CAN BE
LET IT SPILL
WHERE IT WILL.

LOW VOICES.

WE GOTTA
TEA FIGHT
WHY BE NICE?

LOW VOICES.

WHY PRETEND?
WHY NOT SLICE

AND OFFEND?
LET ALL THAT RAGE OUT.
LET THE BOURGEOISIE FIGHT WAGE OUT.
NEVER LET THE TEA FIGHT –

*(Suddenly, **ALGY** and **JAX** enter.)*

JAX. Dearest Gwyn, there you are!

ALGY. My darling Cecile!

CECILE & GWYN. Ernest! *(Catching each other.)* Ernest? *(Moving toward their **ERNESTS**.)* Ernest.

*(**GWYN** rushes to **JAX**.)*

GWYN. This, you horrid little beast is my love, my own. My Ernest!

JAX. Oh my darling Gwyn.

*(**CECILE** rushes to **ALGY**.)*

CECILE. I'm sorry to inform you, that is my guardian Jax Worthing. This is my fiancée, Ernest Worthing.

ALGY. Oh Cecile. You look...delicious.

GWYN. You poor fool! You have been misled. That is my rather worthless cousin, Algy Moncrieff.

CECILE. Algy?

ALGY & JAX. Let me explain.

GWYN. That won't be necessary. I believe, my dearest Cecile, we have both fallen prey to a romantic subterfuge.

ALGY. That sounds dirty, but I merely lied about being their imaginary sibling Ernest.

JAX. And I merely lied about having an imaginary sibling, and then pretended to be them when I was in London.

ALGY. You see, it couldn't be simpler.

CECILE. It certainly sounds so. Doesn't it, Gwyn?

GWYN. Childishly simple. But how best to proceed?

CECILE. Well, I think the only proper thing to do is to offer them some tea?

>(**GWYN** *and* **CECILE** *each grab some bread and butter and cake, and slowly stalk towards* **ALGY** *and* **JAX.***)*

[MUSIC NO. 8A – TEA FIGHT (REPRISE)]

CECILE & GWYN.
WE GOTTA
TEA FIGHT NOW!

WILDES.
THAT'S THE TEA.
THAT'S THE TEA.
THAT'S AS HOT
AS CAN BE.
LET IT SPILL
WHERE IT WILL.

HIGH VOICES.
WE GOTTA

WILDES.
TEA FIGHT

>(**CECILE** *and* **GWYN** *both get* **ALGY** *and* **JAX** *in the face with cake and bread and butter.*)

WHY BE NICE?
WHY PRETEND?
WHY NOT SLICE
AND OFFEND?

WILDES.
LET ALL THAT RAGE OUT.
LET THE BOURGEOISIE FIGHT WAGE OUT.

NEVER LET THE TEA FIGHT END

CECILE & GWYN.
OOH

> (*The* **WILDES** *hand towels to* **CECILE** *and* **GWYN.**)

CECILE. Well, it seems, dearest Gwyn, that we are both engaged to Ernest Worthing.

GWYN. And since there's no Ernest here, we must go out and seek them, don't you think?

CECILE. I do. My own dearest friend, Gwyn.

GWYN. Shall we, my closest companion Cecile?

CECILE. We shall.

> (*They both start to exit.* **ALGY** *follows* **CECILE** *off.*)

ALGY. Cecile, my love. Let me explain. Have you ever heard the term Bunburying?

> (**ALGY** *follows them off.*)

WINCE. Well, I hope you're happy. You've ruined one of the greatest comedic scenes in the entire canon of Western Literature!

SLOUCH. Shhh. Look how sad they are. Jax?

JAX. Yes. I'm sorry. This is all very serious, and I feel like I've hurt the one person I truly loved.

> (**GWYN** *reenters.*)

GWYN. You have. Truly.

WINCE. But this isn't in the script.

GWYN. I know it, but I've lived by the script for far too long. I'm sorry Wince, but I'm taking things into my own hands now. And I am never wrong.

WINCE. With all due respect, Gwyn, this is not the play…

SLOUCH. Doesn't mean it isn't true. Let them have it.

> (**SLOUCH** *takes* **WINCE** *off.*)

JAX. I'm so sorry, Gwyn. I never meant to hurt you. I'm sorry, that I'm not your Ernest.

GWYN. You're not. The Ernest I've known has been always a kind, caring and generous person. And the same could be said of dear Jax Worthing –

[MUSIC NO. 09 – TELL ME]

– or so my dear friend Cecile told me just moments ago. So why would a wonderful person like that have to resort to this kind of duplicity?

> (**WILDES** *enter to watch the love scene they've all been waiting for.*)

> (**GWYN** *doesn't have the words to explain. The* **WILDES** *sing what* **GWYN** *can't yet say.*)

WILDES.
THE WORDS I SPOKE,
CLEVER TO A FAULT,
PUSHED YOU INTO LIES.

> (**JAX** *stands frozen.*)

ABSURD DEMANDS,
RUBBING IN LIKE SALT,
STINGING AS I CLUNG TO YOUR DISGUISE.

GWYN. So there's no Ernest at all?

JAX. None. Just me. I'm sorry. I'm merely one person, who has let you down very badly.

GWYN. But why?

JAX. Well, my dearest Gwyn, you see, I thought I needed to be your Ernest. And Cecile's Jax. And whoever else's anyone so I could be of use to everyone.

GWYN. And what of you? The "you" you truly are? What use can you be to anyone, when you aren't honest about who you are? It's you, that I want to know. You, that I want to love.

> (*As* **GWYN** *is propelled to sing, the* **WILDES** *continue to dance – mirroring their intention.*)

I SEE YOU NOW
MULTITUDES OF YOU,
BEAUTIFUL AND BRAVE.
DON'T PUSH ME OUT
LET ME STAY WITH YOU.
LET'S READ THE WRITING IN THE CAVE.

GWYN & WILDES.

I'M WAITING,
LISTENING
FOR ANYTHING THAT NEEDS CHRISTENING

GWYN.   **WILDES.**

AS PATIENT AS A PRINCE
UNDER A SPELL.   LOVE LOVE
TELL ME WHAT TO CALL   LOVE
   YOU.

WILDES.

TELL ME WHAT TO CALL YOU.

GWYN.

WHISPER IF YOU LIKE.

WILDES.

LOVE
LEAVE THE DOOR CRACKED OPEN

GWYN.

LEAVE THE DOOR CRACKED OPEN

GWYN & WILDES.

QUIETER THAN NIGHT

GWYN.

LET ME HOLD WHAT'S HEAVY,

WILDES.

LET ME HOLD WHAT'S HEAVY.

GWYN & WILDES.

WARM ME WITH YOUR FLAME.

GWYN.	**WILDES.**
TELL ME WHAT TO CALL YOU,	TELL ME,
LOVE. BY ANY NAME.	LOVE.

JAX. I want to be your Ernest.

GWYN. You already are.

JAX.

AFRAID TO BREAK
BOUNDARIES I SET.

JAX & WILDES.

WALK OUTSIDE THE LINES.

GWYN.

YOU'RE SAFE WITH ME,
NEVER NEED TO FRET.

GWYN.	**WILDES.**
LEAVE WHAT YOU NEED TO UNDEFINED.	LEAVE LOVE UNDEFINED.

JAX. Dearest Gwyn, please know that my deception was only meant...

GWYN. To protect me from the truth. I assure you, I need no protection.

(They dance – it's bespoke and beautiful, surprising and tender. There is joy in its careful nature.)

WILDES.

LOVE, LOVE
LOVE, LOVE
LOVE, LOVE

JAX.   **WILDES.**

COULD YOU BE WHAT   LOVE
I NEED?
COULD THE SPELL BE
BROKEN?
NO MORE LIES, NO
DISGUISE.
LOVE OUT IN THE OPEN.

GWYN.

TELL ME WHAT TO   LOVE
CALL YOU.

WILDES.

TELL ME WHAT TO CALL YOU.

GWYN.

WHISPER IF YOU LIKE.

JAX & WILDES.

LOVE

GWYN & WILDES.

LEAVE THE DOOR CRACKED OPEN

JAX.

NO MORE LIES, NO DISGUISE.

GWYN & WILDES.

QUIETER THAN NIGHT.

JAX.

LOVE OUT IN THE OPEN.

GWYN.

LET ME HOLD WHAT'S HEAVY

JAX.

ALL MY FEARS NEED TENDING

GWYN & WILDES.

WARM ME WITH YOUR FLAME.

JAX.

IN A HAPPY ENDING

GWYN.	**WILDES.**	**JAX.**
TELL ME WHAT TO CALL YOU,	TELL ME	IF I TRUST THIS BLUSH OF
	LOVE	LOVE
LOVE.		
	LOVE	
		LOVE

ALL.

LOVE BY ANY NAME.

(In the applause, the **WILDES** *disperse as...)*

Scene Twelve

*(**WINCE** and **SLOUCH** enter.)*

SLOUCH. Oh, isn't Love just wonderful, when it all works out.

WINCE. One imagines, but that is not our story.

SLOUCH. No?

WINCE. Sadly, no.

*(**LADY BRACKNELL** enters with an entourage.)*

[MUSIC NO. 09A – BORN WITH IT (REPRISE)]

LADY BRACKNELL.
HELL OR HIGH WATER..
A MOTHER'S LOVE CANNOT BE MATCHED.
DEVOTION.
ENOUGH TO FILL AN OCEAN.
DO NOT CROSS ME.
MY PROGENY WILL NOT BE SNATCHED.
YOU THINK YOU'LL MARRY?
THAT WON'T BE NECESSARY.
YOU'RE NO CATCH.

PORTRAITS.
WE KNOW THAT YOU'RE NOT

LADY BRACKNELL.
BORN WITH IT

PORTRAITS.
YOU GOT DIDDLY-SQUAT

LADY BRACKNELL.
NOT BORN WITH IT

GWYN. I am engaged, Mamma. To Jax Worthing!

LADY BRACKNELL & PORTRAITS.
NO NO NO NO

GWYN. But Mamma!

LADY BRACKNELL. Gwyn, sit!

PORTRAITS.
FACE THE FACTS!

LADY BRACKNELL.
NOT BORN WITH IT.

PORTRAITS.
GETTING THE AXE!

LADY BRACKNELL.
NOT BORN WITH IT.

PORTRAITS.
SHE'S GOT HER GRANDMOTHER'S TASTE
FOR THE FAMILY WINE.
YOU GOT A NOBODY FACE.

LADY BRACKNELL.
AND I GOT A KICK-LINE!

PORTRAITS.
BRING OUT THE CAKE

(A cake appears – it says "BORN WITH IT.")

LADY BRACKNELL.
BORN WITH IT.

PORTRAITS.
SHIMMY AND SHAKE!
BORN WITH IT.

*(**ALGY** and **CECILE** enter arm in arm,
smiling. **LADY BRACKNELL** sees them and
immediately screeches:)*

LADY BRACKNELL. *WHAT DO YOU THINK YOU'RE DOING HERE???*

PORTRAITS.

BORN –

LADY BRACKNELL. Stop all this whirly-giggery! I fear this country atmosphere is having a most idiotic effect on my lineage.

(They stop.)

ALGY. Oh, hello Aunt Augusta. *(Suddenly panicked.)* AUNT AUGUSTA!

LADY BRACKNELL. Speak of the idiot and they appear.

*(The **PORTRAITS** exit.)*

Algy, how predictable to find you where trouble lurks. I take it, your friend Bunbury, has taken another turn for the worse?

ALGY. Oh, yes! Poor Bunbury died, Aunt Augusta. It was all very tragic, but ultimately necessary.

LADY BRACKNELL. And how, pray, did the poor ailing fellow finally expire?

ALGY. Exploded. Yes, you see, Aunt Augusta, they were found out. I mean to say that doctors found out that Bunbury could not live, so Bunbury died. BOOM!

LADY BRACKNELL. Well, I am glad to hear that Bunbury finally made up his mind. May I ask, who is this young person holding on to Algy in what seems a peculiarly unnecessary manner?

JAX. That is Cecile Cardew, my ward.

CECILE. Algy and I are engaged to be married.

JAX. Cecile is the grandchild of the late Thomas Cardew, my guardian. Thus I am theirs.

LADY BRACKNELL. And I presume that this young person is not at all connected with any of the larger railway stations? May one inquire if Miss Cardew has any fortune to speak of?

CECILE. Oh, about a hundred and thirty thousand pounds in funds.

LADY BRACKNELL. Come over here, child. Your dress is sadly simple and your hair seems almost as Nature might have left it, but there are distinct possibilities in your profile. The nose a little higher dear. Style largely depends on how the nose is worn.

      *(***CECILE** *keeps turning.)*

ALGY. Aunt Augusta, Cecile is the sweetest, and dearest person in the whole world. And I don't care tuppence about social possibilities.

LADY BRACKNELL. Never speak disrespectfully of Society, Algy. Only people who can't get into it do that.

      *(***LADY BRACKNELL** *gets up to inspect* **CECILE**.*)*

Now, my dear child, you must know that Algy can depend on very little besides his debts. He has nothing but looks everything.

ALGY. But who, being loved, is poor?

LADY BRACKNELL. You are, Algy. And thanks to lovely Cecile, perhaps you will be no longer.

CECILE. Anything for you, Algy. I adore you.

ALGY. Even with my unfortunate name?

CECILE. Much like the pond scum, you have grown on me.

LADY BRACKNELL. How fortunate. A love match, thank goodness you'll both have enough money to survive it. You may kiss me, Cecile. I give my full approval.

(**CECILE** *starts toward* **LADY BRACKNELL**, *but is stopped by* **JAX**.)

JAX. I beg your pardon for interrupting, Lady Bracknell, but this engagement is quite out of the question.

CECILE. *(Suddenly loud.)* Wait, what?

JAX. I do not approve of Algy's moral character. Why this very afternoon, they obtained admission to my house under the false pretense of being my sibling and succeeded in alienating the affections of my ward.

CECILE. *(Confused.)* No, they didn't.

JAX. *(Hinting to go along with it.)* But yes, they did, Cecile. Check your diary.

CECILE. *(Suddenly loud.)* Yes they did!

(**CECILE** *pushes* **ALGY** *away*.)

You're terrible.

ALGY. I thought you liked me for that.

LADY BRACKNELL. That was rather naughty of you, Algy. However, after careful consideration I have decided to overlook dear Algy's conduct. I find that I often must.

JAX. That is very generous of you, Lady Bracknell, however I do not overlook it. And I do not give my consent. I'm sorry, Cecile.

CECILE. *(Loud.)* You have broken my heart!

LADY BRACKNELL. How cruel, you are. To spoil the dreams of a beautiful young person in love.

ALGY. *(Very upset.)* I know, and Cecile's sad too!

JAX. I'm afraid it can't be helped. Unless?

WILDES. Unless.

JAX. I imagine, I could see my way toward giving my consent to Cecile's marrying Algy, if you, Lady Bracknell would agree to my marrying Gwyn.

GWYN. Oh, Ernest!

WILDES. Ernest.

LADY BRACKNELL. What you propose is quite out of the question. Come along Gwyn, we shall return to London at once. At least there, manners and courtesies are observed to their absurdest of conclusions.

Scene Thirteen

(**SLOUCH** *enters.*)

SLOUCH. Well, the vicar says the fonts lay at the ready for the christenings. Shall we have two dunks or one?

LADY BRACKNELL. Prism! Not in twenty-five years did I ever imagine I would see your face again.

SLOUCH. Who? Me?

LADY BRACKNELL. (*Overly dramatic.*) Prism!

[MUSIC NO. 10 – WHAT A SHAME]

Where is the baby?

ALL.
THE BABY!
THE BABY!
THE BABY!

SLOUCH.
WHAT?!

ALL.
THE BABY!
THE BABY!
THE BABY!

(**SLOUCH** *opens the script and flips pages trying to find out about this baby.*)

LADY BRACKNELL. Twenty-five years ago you left Lord Bracknell's house in charge of a perambulator that contained a very precious babe. With this child, you never returned. Prism, where is that child?

SLOUCH. (*Finding the page.*) Oh yes –

THE BABY.
WHAT A –

WILDES.

SHHH-SHAME!

SLOUCH.

WHAT A –

WILDES.

SHHH-SHAME!

SLOUCH. The one I lost. Twenty-five years ago, on my way to the park.

WHAT A –

WILDES.

SHHH...

LADY BRACKNELL. *(Interrupting.)* Well, Prism, elucidate.

SLOUCH. No thanks, I'm not hungry. But I will sing. C major,* please.

> *(Lights change, and* **SLOUCH** *strikes a dramatic form.)*

LADY BRACKNELL. Oh for heaven's sake.

SLOUCH.

IN MY YOUNGER DAYS, I LIVED-IN
AS A NURSEMAID TO THE RICH.
I RECALL THAT LONDON MORNING.
IT WAS SUNNY FOR A SWITCH.
I GOT OUT THE BABY BUGGY
AND A BITTY BABY STOLE
AND I TOOK MY BONNY BABY
FOR A BITTY BABY STROLL.

> *(The* **WILDES** *create a sense of the London morning.)*

WILLS. Allo, Governor!

---

* This line should reflect whatever key **SLOUCH** sings in.

OSCAR. Pip-Pip! Cheerio!

WILDES.
> THE BABY
> THE BABY
> THE BA–A–ABY

SLOUCH.
> WHAT A –

WILDES.
> SHHH ...

WILDE SOLOIST. *(As the baby.)*
> WAHHHH!

SLOUCH.
> WHAT A –

WILDES.
> SHHH ...

WILDE SOLOIST. *(As Eliza Doolittle.)* Flowers for Sale!

SLOUCH.
> WHAT A –

WILDES.	**WILDE SOLOIST.**
SHHHHHHHHH...	Fancy a spotted dick?

WILDES.
> SHAME...

SLOUCH.
> BITTY BABY WAS SO HAPPY
> JUST TO LIE IN BUGGY BLISS.
> GOO GOO GA GA
> OFF TO SLEEPY TIME
> WITH NO MORE THAN A KISS
> SO I SAT DOWN WITH MY HANDBAG
> AND MY EYE UPON THE CHILD

> (**SLOUCH** *picks up the Wilde fairy tale book.)*

SLOUCH.

AND I OPENED UP THE FAIRY TALES –

(The book opens and the tone shifts into the world of "Wilde.")

OF DEAR OL' OSCAR WILDE.

*(***WILDES*** pass by* **SLOUCH,** *now quoting Fairy tales of Oscar Wilde.)*

SPERANZA.

OH OH.

WILLS.

OH OH.

WILDE.

OH OH.

WILDES.

"ABOVE THE CITY STOOD
A STATUE OF A PRINCE"

SLOUCH.

BECOME...

WILDES.

"CHILDREN IN THE GARDEN
PLAY BENEATH THE QUINCE."

WILDES.

THE LANGUAGE SET APART
VICTORIAN AND QUEER,
EXPOSED A BEATING HEART
THAT ECHOED
A VOICE RINGING CLEAR

SLOUCH.

THE CASTLES AND THE ROSES

WILDES.

HERE

SLOUCH.

THE GIANTS AND THE NOSES

WILDES.

HERE...

> (**SLOUCH** *gets more and more lost in the fairy*
> *tales.)*

SLOUCH.	**WILDES.**
THE HIJINKS AND THE	AH
SLY WINKS	

SLOUCH.

AND THE WILDNESS WILDE EXPOSES –

LADY BRACKNELL. Slouch!!

THE BABY!

SLOUCH.

THE BABY????

WILDES.

THE BABY!!!

WHAT A

SLOUCH.	**WILDES.**
NO NEED FOR YOU	SHHH...
YELLING IT	
I'M GETTING TO THE	SHAME!
TELLING IT!	

SLOUCH.

THE FAIRY TALES HAD SPUN THEIR WEB

AND TIME BEGAN TO SLIP.

AS THE THUNDER CLOUDS EXPLODED

INTO DRIBBLE DRIBBLE DRIP.

> (*The* **WILDES** *start to notice it's raining and*
> *slowly fill the stage with umbrellas.)*

ENSEMBLE.

DRIP, DRIP, DRIP, DRIP,
DRIP, DRIP.

DRIP, DRIP, DRIP, DRIP,
DRIP, DRIP.

WILDE SOLOIST.

Raining in England?!

FINGAL.

Who could believe it?

SLOUCH.

IN THE MELEE OF THE RAIN DAY
I WAS WAYLAID FROM THE PRAM
AS THE DELUGE AND THE CHAOS SPREAD

(All the **WILDES** *open umbrellas.)*

FROM HERE TO BUCKINGHAM!

(The **WILDES***' umbrellas create a wall of black, twirling around.* **SLOUCH** *and* **WILDE** *disappear under the cover of umbrellas and pop up again in different spots.)*

SLOUCH & WILDES.

WHAT A SHHH–
SHAME
WHAT A SHHH–
SHAME
WHAT A –

*(***WILDE** *appears in another pocket, and cries out to* **SLOUCH***.)*

WILDE. *(As baby.)*

WAHHHH!

WILDES.

SHHH...
WHAT A –

WILDE SOLOIST.

WAHHHH!

WILDES.
WHAT A SHAME

> (**WINCE** *enters, furious.* **WINCE** *immediately starts turning down umbrellas.*)

SLOUCH.
BITTY BABY! WHERE WAS BABY?!
AND WHERE WAS THE MISSING PRAM?

LADY BRACKNELL.
THE BABY...

SLOUCH.
I COULD NEVER FACE M' LADY,
SO THIS NURSEMAID BETTER SCRAM.

LADY BRACKNELL.
THE BABY...

SLOUCH.

	WILDES.
FOR SOMEHOW THE BABY	
IS LOST IN THE SHUFFLE	
THE RUFFLES OF FABRIC	
WERE LOST IN THE SEA	
OF RUBBER GALOSHES	DRIP
THAT SLOSH AND	DRIP
UMBRELLAS	
THAT HUSTLE AND BUSTLE	DRIP
TO AFTERNOON TEA	DRIP
I HURRIED MYSELF	OH
TO VICTORIA STATION	
I PURCHASED A TICKET	
ONE-WAY TO THE MOORS.	
DONNED THE FACADE OF A	OH
CRANKY OLD TUTOR	
WHO HATES ALL THE	
DRAMA HER TUTEE	
EXPLORES.	

WILDES.

WHAT?

WILDE SOLOIST.

SHHHH

WILDES. *(Quiet.)*

WHAT A –

SLOUCH.

SUCH IS THE BUS'NESS	**WILDES.**
OF STORY DEVICES	SHAME
WHILE PLOTTING A	
FARCE	
THAT DEPENDS ON A	
NAME.	
HIJINKS AND	SHAME!
HOODWINKS	
AND ALL KINDS OF VICES	
FOR BREAKING WITH	
NORMS	
IS A DANGEROUS GAME	

SLOUCH & WILDES.

ASK OSCAR WILDE

AND HE'LL TELL YOU SAME!

WILDE. What?

SLOUCH.

FAMOUS AND INFAMOUS	
DASHING AND	
DANGEROUS	**WILDES.**
WHAT AN UNBEARABLE	WHAT.
TALE OF TERRIBLE	A.
SHAME!	SHAME!

(The number ends. **SLOUCH** *bows deeply. The* **WILDES** *bow as well.)*

(Everyone is very proud. Wasn't that fun?)

WINCE. What in the fingal o'flahertie is happening here?!!

(**LADY BRACKNELL** *and* **WINCE** *both seethe.*)

Explain yourself.

SLOUCH. We made a beautiful climax to the play!

WINCE. Not this play. Not this play by Oscar Wilde. No, you most certainly did not. You were given but one task, Slouch. To read the lines, as they were written!

SLOUCH. I was just trying to help.

WINCE. Help? Oscar Wilde does not need your help. He needs your obedience. He needs you to follow the script, wherein Wilde makes some of his most brilliant observations about the state of the British novel.

CECILE. Book humor. Thrilling.

WINCE. How very dare you?

[MUSIC NO. 11 – WIDER SPECTRUM (REPRISE)]

This man was a genius. This man was ahead of his time. We can't perform this crowning achievement of Oscar Wilde's with all this nincompoopery!

ALGY. Ooh, you said a bad word.

SLOUCH. We're trying to honor the man but also honor ourselves. Why can't we do both?

JAX.

We've been doing both this whole time. This whole time, I've thought that to please all, I had to be all.	**WILDES**.
	ON A WIDER SPECTRUM
But we cannot be all, we must be only ourselves.	

WINCE. But you cannot alter this work. This masterpiece. The author would never approve.

SLOUCH. Well, why don't we ask them?

(**OSCAR** *and* **WILDE** *step forward, with all the* **WILDES** *behind them.*)

OSCAR. We're Oscar

FINGAL. Fingal

O'FLAHERTIE. O'Flahertie

WILLS. Wills.

WILDE. Wilde. The author of this charming play.

WINCE. All of you?

WILDES.
YES.

ALGY & WINCE.
ON A WIDE–

CECILE & GWYN.
ON A WIDE–

SLOUCH.
ON A WIDE–

OSCAR & FINGAL.
ON A WIDE–

O'FLAHERTIE & WILLS.
ON A WIDE–

WILDE & SPERANZA.
ON A WIDE–

ALL.
–ER SPECTRUM

JAX.
NOTHING'S OUT OF RANGE.

SLOUCH. This is the complete works of Oscar Wilde. And so much more happens.

WINCE. Yes, to the author, but not in the play!

JAX.

TRUTHS CAN COEXIST.

SLOUCH.

FAIRYTALES CAN SHIFT.

JAX & SLOUCH.

WE CAN PLAY IT BY THE BOOK AND MAKE IT STRANGE.

WILDES.

WHAT IF IT OPENS LIKE A RAINBOW?

WINCE. Surely we can separate one's life away from one's art?

JAX. That seems a little difficult, Wince, when one's art is one's life at the present.

SLOUCH. My dear Wince, the great appeal of the theatre is that it is a living breathing thing.

WILDES.

THE PLAY CAN OPEN LIKE A RAINBOW -

JAX.

OH THE PLAY CAN OPEN LIKE A RAINBOW -

(The music becomes drier, sparse.)

WINCE. But we are doing this specific play.

SLOUCH. Yes, but in our specific way. In our specific time. Honoring both the play, and the person who wrote it.

O'FLAHERTIE. He'd be so surprised to know we'd being doing the play at all.

SLOUCH. Just a few weeks after this play opened, Oscar Wilde was arrested.

WILDES.

SHHH...

SLOUCH. For the great sin of being exactly who he was.

GWYN. And loving exactly who he loved.

WILDES.

SHHH...

WINCE. Yes, and that is a tragedy. But this play is not a tragedy. This play is...

ENSEMBLE.	**WILDES.**
SHHH...	MMM

SLOUCH. A masterwork as you say, Wince. One of the greatest plays the world has ever known, and yet, poor dear Oscar never got to know any of that success.

ALGY. Oh my dear, why?

WILDES.

SHHH...

SLOUCH. He was sentenced to two years hard labor.

FINGAL. Prisoner: C. 33.

WILDES.

...SHAME

OSCAR. "In Reading jaol (jail) by Reading Town, there is a pit of..."

WILDES.

SHHH...

OSCAR. Two years later, he was dead in a rented room in Paris.

WILDE. "Either that wallpaper goes, or I do."

SLOUCH. Even to the end, his wit remained.

WINCE. But it's the wit these people have come to see. The wit you were meant to produce.

SLOUCH. Well, how lucky for them and for us that we can give them all this truth with it. We're not destroying the world of Oscar Wilde, we're opening him up to ours.

WILDES.

SO SMALL AND SHORT

THERE'S A WIDER SPECTRUM

SLOUCH. Wince, we live in a world beyond Wilde's dreams.

WILDES.

WIDER THAN WE KNEW.

WILDE. *(To* **WINCE**.*)* You lose nothing in my being me, but perhaps gain the freedom to know you can be you as well.

WINCE. Is that Wilde?

SLOUCH. No, but it sounds like them, doesn't it?

WILDES.

LIES SOMETIMES REVEAL

SOMETHING THAT'S MORE REAL,

JAX.

SOMETHING YOU DON'T DARE ADMIT

JAX & WILDES.

UNTIL IT'S TRUE.

WILDE. To love one's self is to begin a lifelong romance.

WILDES.

THE PLAY CAN OPEN LIKE A RAINBOW

WINCE. Yes. I see –

LADY BRACKNELL. What?? What does everyone see???

WILDES.

SHHH...

LADY BRACKNELL. This is preposterous! To think that I, the seminal lead of this piece...

ALGY. Oh Aunt Augusta, you are not.

[MUSIC NO. 12 – WORTHY]

LADY BRACKNELL. Everyone comes for Lady Bracknell, and you know it!

WINCE. I'm sorry, Jax, I see now that I was trying to hold on to something...

JAX.
> BEFORE YOU SAY IT
> BEFORE WE TIE THE LOOSE ENDS.
> HANG IN THE BALANCE,
> BEFORE WE MAKE AMENDS.
> WE ARE, I AM, YOU ARE WORTHY –

LADY BRACKNELL. *(Protesting.)* We are here to discuss marriage and respectability, love has nothing to do with it, whatsoever.

ALGY. I think that's where you're wrong, Lady Bracknell... Love is at the root of it all.

SLOUCH. Or must be.

GWYN.
> MAYBE WE MARRY

CECILE.
> OH

JAX.
> MAYBE WE'RE GONNA LIVE THAT BLISS.

GWYN.
> MAYBE WE PART WAYS

ALGY.
> OH.

GWYN & JAX.
> BUT LET'S HOLD ON TO THIS.

JAX.
WE ARE, I AM, YOU ARE WORTHY.

GWYN & JAX.
WE ARE

JAX.
I AM

GWYN.
YOU ARE

GWYN & JAX.
WORTHY

JAX.
WORTHY OF LOVE.

GWYN & JAX.
WORTHY OF LOVE.

WINCE. If we cling too tightly to who we were.

SLOUCH. We'll never give ourselves enough room to grow into who we are.

JAX & CECILE.
KEEP YOUR CONFESSION

ALGY, GWYN, SLOUCH & WINCE.
OH

JAX & CECILE.
TIED IN A TIDY BOW.

ALGY, GWYN, SLOUCH & WINCE.
OH

JAX & CECILE.
THERE'S NO CONFESSION

ALGY, CECILE, SLOUCH & WINCE.
OH

JAX & CECILE.
THAT TAKES IN WHAT I KNOW

CECILE & ALGY.
WE ARE

CECILE.
I AM

ALGY.
YOU ARE WORTHY

SLOUCH & WINCE.
WE ARE

SLOUCH.
I AM

WINCE.
YOU ARE

SLOUCH & WINCE.
WORTHY

JAX, GWYN, ALGY, CECILE, SLOUCH & WINCE.
WORTHY OF LOVE.

JAX & SLOUCH.
WORTHY

JAX, GWYN, ALGY, CECILE, SLOUCH & WINCE.
WORTHY OF LOVE.

CECILE, GWYN, JAX & SLOUCH.
WE'RE ALL MADE OF THE BAGGAGE WE CARRY.
BURDENED BY OUR BURIED SECRETS, BUT MAYBE

GWYN & JAX.
WE ARE

SLOUCH.
I AM

JAX, GWYN, ALGY, CECILE, SLOUCH & WINCE.
YOU ARE WORTHY
WORTHY OF LOVE.

WINCE.
WORTHY,

CECILE.
OH,

JAX, GWYN, ALGY, CECILE, SLOUCH & WINCE.
WORTHY OF LOVE.
WORTHY OF LOVE.

JAX.
WE'RE ALL JUST SOULS TRYING TO SURVIVE

WILDES.
OOH

JAX, CECILE & WILDES.
LYING

JAX & CECILE.	**WILDES.**
ILL AT EASE,	OOH

ALL.
UNTIL WE FLING OUR ARMS WIDE
AND WE ARRIVE
WE ARE, I AM, YOU ARE WORTHY

CECILE, GWYN, JAX & SLOUCH.
WE ARE ALL MADE OF BAGGAGE WE CARRY.
BURDENED BY OUR BURIED SECRETS, BUT

ALL.
MAYBE
WE ARE, I AM, YOU ARE WORTHY,
WORTHY OF LOVE.
OH, OH,

WILDES.
WE ARE

JAX.

I AM

GWYN.

YOU ARE

ALL.

WORTHY.

> *(Applause.)*

SLOUCH. Would you like to finish the play?

WINCE. *(Nodding like a child.)* I would, if that's alright.

LADY BRACKNELL. Finally! It is high time someone took this whole bumbling disgrace in hand, why in my day...

GWYN. Mamma, be quiet.

LADY BRACKNELL. Gwyn, what is the meaning of this impertinence!

GWYN. Mamma, Quiet! Mamma, Sit!

> **(LADY BRACKNELL** *sits.)*

Good Mamma.

SLOUCH. The floor is yours.

> **(WINCE** *steps forward, clipboard away for the first time. Scared, but happy to know they are supported.)*

WINCE. Prism admits to leaving the baby in the handbag.

SLOUCH. I got mixed up.

WINCE. The handbag is collected.

> *(One of the* **WILDES** *hands the infamous handbag to* **SLOUCH.***)*

SLOUCH. It seems to be mine. On the lock, there, are my initials.

JAX. Prism, more is restored to you than this handbag. I was the baby you placed in it!

(**JAX** *embraces* **SLOUCH***!*)

SLOUCH. There is the lady who can tell you who you really are.

(**SLOUCH** *points to* **LADY BRACKNELL**.*)*

ALL. Lady Bracknell!

LADY BRACKNELL. Yes, who did you think? I'm afraid the news that I have to give you will not altogether please you. You are the son of my poor sister, Mrs. Moncrieff.

ALGY. Mummy?

JAX. Then, Algy is my sibling. I always knew I had a sibling.

GWYN. Oh, my darling, my own. My cousin?!

WINCE. It was a different time.

JAX. Let's not quibble that point at the moment, Gwyn. Aunt Augusta, at the time when Prism left me in the handbag, had I been christened already?

LADY BRACKNELL. Being the eldest child you were christened after your father.

SLOUCH. Ernest. Your father's name was Ernest!

WILDES. Ernest.

LADY BRACKNELL. Yes, I remember now that the General was called Ernest, I knew I had some particular reason for disliking the name.

GWYN. Ernest! My own Ernest! I felt from the first that you could have no other name!

JAX. Gwyn, it is a terrible thing to find out suddenly that all my life I have been speaking nothing but the truth. Can you forgive me?

GWYN. I can. I have.

ALGY. Cecile! At last!

JAX. Gwyn! At last!

LADY BRACKNELL. It seems you are all displaying signs of triviality.

JAX. On the contrary, Aunt Augusta, I've now realized for the first time in my life, the vital Importance of Being...

ENSEMBLE. ERNEST!

JAX. I've never felt a name fit me more.

> (*The* **WILDES** *begin to move everyone out to prepare for the finale. Only* **SLOUCH** *and* **WINCE** *are still onstage.*)

Scene Fourteen

SLOUCH. Oh I love when they say the title of the play! And I love a happy ending.

WINCE. Of course you do. But...

SLOUCH. DON'T RUIN IT!

(They're both shocked at the outburst, but they agree to move on.)

WINCE. And so our young couples were wed.

*(The **WILDES** pair off and form a procession.)*

WILDE. Keep Love in your life.

WILLS. A life without it is like a sunglass garden when the flowers are dead.

WINCE. All the society papers wrote of the momentous event.

O'FLAHERTIE. There is no feeling more comforting or consoling...

OSCAR. Then knowing you are right next to the one you love.

WINCE. The dignified matron wore a tasteful grey.

*(**LADY BRACKNELL** enters in a beautiful grey dress.)*

LADY BRACKNELL. One should absorb the color of life, but one should never remember its details.

FINGAL. Love is a mutual understanding between two fools.

WILLS. When you really want love, you will find it waiting for you.

*(**CECILE** comes down the aisle walking arm in arm with **ALGY**.)*

SLOUCH. Cecile Cardew married Algy Moncreiff of Grosvenor Square.

CECILE. But I just call them Trouble.

ALGY. I couldn't think of a name more fitting.

*(**GWYN** walks now with **JAX (ERNEST)**, who wears a large E on their jacket.)*

WINCE. And so Gwyn Fairfax wearing the most dazzling white...

LADY BRACKNELL. Chosen by their mother.

WINCE. Married Ernest Worthing, of Hertfordshire.

SLOUCH. How does it feel, Ernest?

JAX. Singularly wonderful.

WINCE. Thus we all see the Importance of being Earnest.

[MUSIC NO. 13 – X MARKS THE SPOT]

*(Two **WILDES** bring out the sign again.)*

WINCE. *(To **JAX**.)* I beg your pardon, but may I borrow your E? To correct the sign.

JAX. I should think you'd leave it. X is the great unknown, is it not? Let each who seek it, find their own way to whatever sort of Ernest they would like to be.

GWYN. I have the best one, anyway.

ALL.
X!

WILDES.
YOU ARE THE ANSWER YOU NEEDED.

ALL.

X!

WILDES.

YOU KNOW THE UNIVERSE YOU HOLD.
INSIDE, AROUND PLANETS OF GRIEF
IN RELIEF,
YOU ARE STARDUST,

ALL.

BRIGHT AND BOLD.

SPERANZA.

YOU KNOW
WHERE YOU STAND

**OSCAR, FINGAL,
O'FLAHERTIE & WILLS.**   **SPERANZA.**

YOU HOLD THE MAP   OH
CHARTING WHERE
    YOU'LL LAND.

                    X

MARKS THE SPOT,
YOU STAND HERE TODAY,
THE PATH IS UNKNOWN
BUT X MARKS THE WAY BACK.
X HOLDS YOUR GROUND
THE ROOT WHERE YOU START TO GROW.
YOU CAN GO AND RETURN
BECAUSE YOU ALWAYS KNOW

SOLO VOICE.

X

SOLO VOICE.

X

SOLO VOICE.

X

OSCAR, FINGAL, O'FLAHERTIE & WILLS.
X MARKS THE SPOT.

LADY BRACKNELL. Though your courtship has been less than ideal, I wish you both happiness and health in marriage.

GWYN. Thank you, Mamma.

JAX. Yes, thank you, Mamma.

LADY BRACKNELL. Now that I look at you, I see so clearly your father's nose. My Gwyn is a very lucky person.

GWYN. I know. I am.

LADY BRACKNELL. Now all that remains is to get you on the right side of Belgrave Square.

ALL.
X!

JAX.
YOUR DEEPEST SECRETS ARE SACRED.

ALL.
X!

GWYN.
YOU HONOR WHO YOU CHOOSE TO TELL.

CECILE & GWYN.
AND THEN, WHEN YOU'RE READY TO SHINE

CECILE.
YOU'LL BE FINE.

CECILE & ALGY.
YOU GOT STARDUST

CECILE, ALGY, GWYN & JAX.
THAT'S YOUR SPELL.

SLOUCH.
WHO KNOWS WHERE YOU'LL LAND?

ALL.

YOU HOLD THE MAP.
SO IT'S IN YOUR HANDS.
X MARKS THE SPOT,
YOU STAND HERE TODAY,
THE PATH IS UNKNOWN
BUT X MARKS THE WAY BACK.
X HOLDS YOUR GROUND
THE ROOT WHERE YOU START TO GROW.
YOU CAN GO AND RETURN
TO THE TRUTH THAT YOU KNOW

SOLO VOICE.

X

SOLO VOICE.

X

SOLO VOICE.

X

ALL.

X MARKS X MARKS

FINGAL.

THIS IS THE PLACE WHERE YOU STAND.
DRAW A LINE IN THE SAND.
THIS IS HEALING.

OSCAR, FINGAL, WILLS & SPERANZA.

YOU'RE STILL SHAKEN FROM HOW IT'S
REVEALING THE LESSON YOU NEARLY FORGOT.

WILDES.

THAT NO, DEAR, YOU ARE NOT
THE ONLY, THE LONELY, THE SILO YOU THOUGHT.

ALL.

'CAUSE SURPRISE,
WHEN YOU OPEN YOUR EYES –

LOOK! SEE!
YOU NEVER HAVE BEEN,
NEVER WILL BE AGAIN.
YOU HAVE BRETHREN.
KIN, TIGHT-KNIT AND SEWN.
TURNS OUT – NO LIES –
TURNS OUT – JUST WIDE SKIES!
TURNS OUT –
TURNS OUT – YOU ARE NOT ALONE.

   (Tenderly.)

X MARKS THE SPOT,
THE STAND THAT YOU TAKE.
THE CHOICE TO GO ON.
THE SPACE THAT YOU'RE MAKING.
X HOLDS YOUR GROUND
IT'S WORN LIKE A BATTLE SCAR.
YOU CAN GO AND RETURN
'CAUSE YOU KNOW WHO YOU ARE.

SOLO VOICE. *(Riff.)*
YOU KNOW WHO YOU ARE

SOLO VOICE. *(Riff.)*	**ALL.**
YEA!	X MARKS X MARKS
YEA!	OH

   *(The **WILDES** and the **COUPLES** start peeling off and exiting, to begin their happy lives.)*

GROUP 1.	**GROUP 2.**
X MARKS THE SPOT,	BECOME
YOU STAND HERE TODAY,	
THE PATH IS UNKNOWN BUT	OH BECOME
X MARKS THE WAY BACK.	X MARKS THE WAY
X MARKS THE SPOT,	BECOME
YOU STAND HERE TODAY,	BECOME YOUR SELF.

<table>
<tr><td>

GROUP 1.
    THE PATH IS UNKNOWN
        BUT
    X MARKS THE WAY BACK.
    X MARKS THE SPOT,
    X MARKS THE SPOT,

</td><td>

GROUP 2.
BECOME

BECOME YOUR SELF.
BECOME

</td></tr>
</table>

ALL.
    WE ARE
    I AM
    YOU ARE WORTHY

SLOUCH. We did a very good play, Wince.

WINCE. Thanks to you, Slouch.

SLOUCH. *(Taking* **WINCE***'s hand.)* Please, call me [Emily].*

ENSEMBLE.
    WE ARE WORTHY OF LOVE

        (**SLOUCH** *and* **WINCE** *go off hand in hand.*
        The play is over.)

The End

---

*Or whatever the actor's first name is.

www.ingramcontent.com/pod-product-compliance
Lightning Source LLC
Chambersburg PA
CBHW071927130726

47909CB00014B/2621